The Boxcar Children® Mysteries

THE MYSTERY OF THE HIDDEN BEACH

created by
GERTRUDE CHANDLER WARNER

Illustrated by Charles Tang

ALBERT WHITMAN & Company
Morton Grove, Illinois

Library of Congress Cataloging-in-Publication Data

Warner, Gertrude Chandler, 1890-
The mystery of the hidden beach / created by Gertrude Chandler Warner;
illustrated by Charles Tang.
p. cm. — (The Boxcar children mysteries)
Summary: While visiting the Florida Keys, the Aldens encounter suspicious
characters, strange incidents at night, and a plot to steal valuable coral.
ISBN 0-8075-5403-0 (hardcover).
ISBN 0-8075-5404-9 (paperback).
[1. Florida Keys (Fla.)–Fiction. 2. Coral reefs and islands–Fiction.
3. Mystery and detective stories.]
I. Tang, Charles, ill. II. Title. III. Series: Warner, Gertrude
Chandler, 1890-   Boxcar children mysteries.
PZ7.C359615 My   1994   94-5674
[Fic]–dc20   CIP
                                                    AC

Cover art by David Cunningham.

Contents

CHAPTER 1

Welcome to Camp Coral

"Are we almost there?" Violet asked eagerly. She was wedged in the front seat between Grandfather and Henry as the rental car sped along the Overseas Highway toward Key West, Florida.

"We just passed Key Largo," Grandfather told her, "so we have another couple of hours to go."

"And we have a lot more Keys to go," Jessie piped up from the back seat. "Sugarloaf Key, Eagle Key, Big Pine Key . . ." She reeled off the names from a map that Soo Lee had spread across her lap.

"I hope we'll be at Camp Coral in time for dinner," said Benny, who was six. He loved to eat.

"The names are so pretty," Soo Lee said. She stared out the window at the turquoise water that inched right up to the narrow ribbon of highway. The silvery blue-green Atlantic Ocean was on the left, and the Gulf of Mexico was on the right.

"I'm glad you came with us, Soo Lee," Violet said.

"So am I." Soo Lee was a seven-year-old Korean girl who had been adopted by Joe and Alice Alden, the Boxcar children's aunt and uncle. She was looking forward to sharing adventures with her new cousins.

"I think we'll see a lot of the islands and keys at Camp Coral," Jessie assured her. "They have fourteen boats, and we'll be on the water every day." Jessie, who was twelve, was the most organized of the four

Boxcar children, and she had read the camp handbook from cover to cover.

"I'll be on the water, too," Grandfather said. "Jake loves to fish and I expect we'll be out catching blue marlin and snapper for dinner." He had already explained to the children that he would be visiting his friend on Upper Matecumbe Key while they were at camp for a week.

"I bet you'll have fun, Grandfather," Violet said, resting her hand on Grandfather's shoulder. Ten-year-old Violet Alden was a shy, sensitive child, who was very attached to her grandfather. She remembered the days when she and her sister and brothers were orphans, living in a boxcar, and Grandfather had found them and given them a real home.

It was late afternoon when Henry, who was fourteen, spotted a small green sign. "That's it," he said excitedly. "Turn here for Camp Coral, Grandfather." They left the highway and headed down a narrow dirt road bordered by a tropical jungle of mangrove trees and palms. A pair of white herons streaked across the sky, and a small deer darted across the road into a thicket.

A few minutes later, they arrived at a collection of white stucco buildings nestled at the edge of a dazzling blue ocean. Two giant palms framed a nautical-looking sign: WELCOME TO CAMP CORAL. A piece of fishermen's net was draped over one corner, and a thick coil of rope formed the words.

"We're here!" Benny shouted. As soon as Grandfather pulled into the parking lot, Benny scrambled out of the car. Jessie and Soo Lee were right behind him.

"It's just like I pictured it," Violet said, turning to help unload the luggage from the trunk. A group of campers were paddling kayaks close to the shore, and two young girls walked by in wet suits. They were carrying goggles and flippers, and one of them waved to her.

"Why are they dressed like that?" Benny asked curiously.

"They're probably going snorkeling," Grandfather told him. "Or maybe even scuba diving. They teach both here at the camp."

"And we teach a lot of other fun things," a young woman said, walking up to them. She was wearing cut-off shorts and a red T-shirt with the word STAFF printed on it. "I'm Melanie, the activity director," she said, sticking out her hand to Grandfather. "And you must be the Aldens."

Grandfather shook Melanie's hand and introduced everyone. Then a loud bark made Melanie turn in surprise. "Oops," she said, reaching down to pat a friendly-looking collie. "I forgot to introduce Bingo. He's the camp mascot."

"We have a dog back home," Benny said. "His name is Watch."

Melanie smiled at him. "Then I'll give you a special assignment, Benny. You can give Bingo his doggie treat every day after dinner. Would you like that?"

"You bet!"

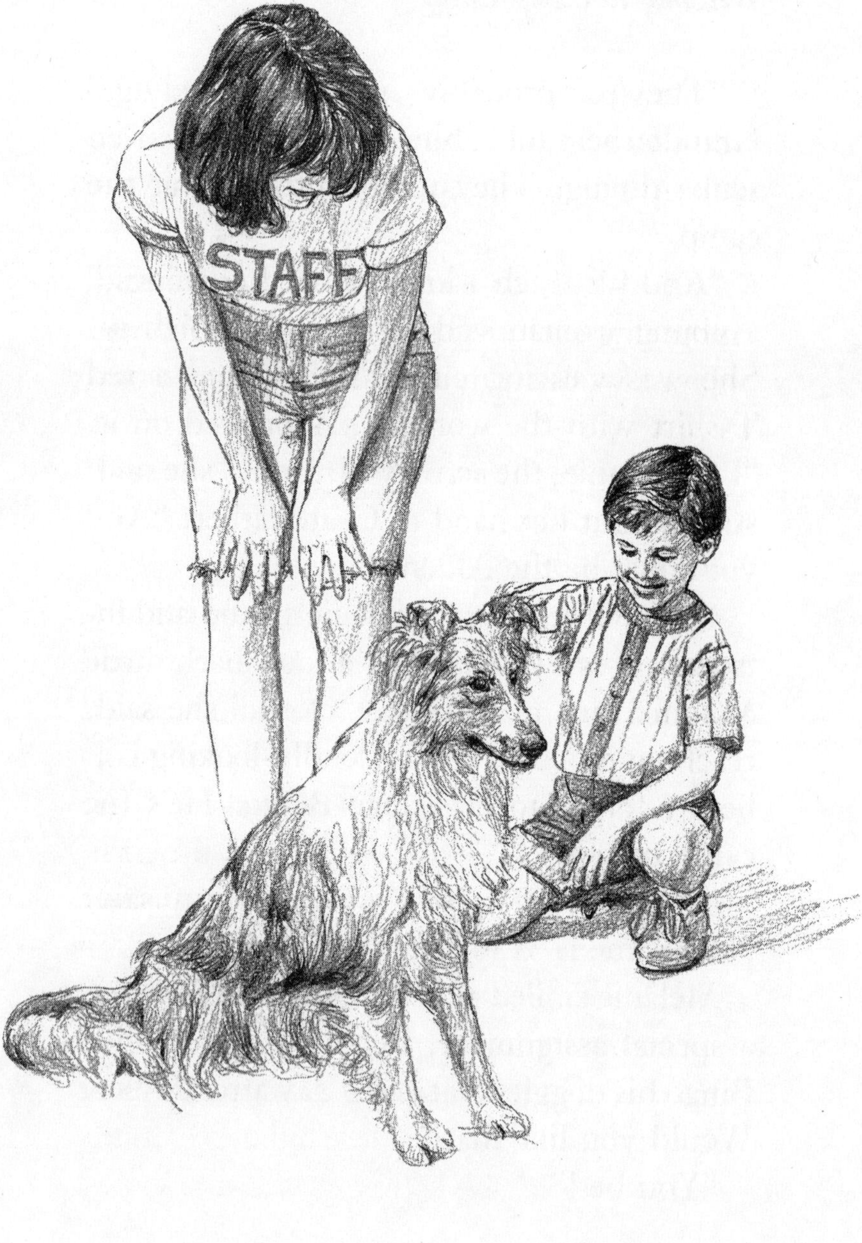
STAFF

"Now, after you say your good-byes, I'll take you to your cabins." She bent down to pick up one of the duffel bags lying next to the car.

"Good-bye, children," Grandfather said, embracing each of the children in a big hug. "Have a wonderful time, and I'll see you next week."

"Good-bye, Grandfather," Jessie said, somewhat sadly.

"We'll miss you!" Violet added.

Grandfather started the engine and the children waved until the blue car had rounded a turn in the dirt road and was out of sight.

"Ready, everyone?" Melanie asked. "The boys' cabins are on the right, and the girls' are straight ahead." Everyone trooped after her as she headed for a long white building and tapped on the door. A moment later, they stepped into a cheerful room lined with bunk beds. A braided rug was on the floor and fresh muslin curtains billowed at the windows. "Nobody's here at the moment. I guess everyone's in class or doing an activity."

"In class?" Benny said, surprised. "I thought this was a camp."

Melanie laughed. "Sometimes you have to learn things before you can do them." She helped Henry and Benny unload their backpacks on two empty beds, and then pointed to the window. "Take a look outside."

Violet pushed aside the curtains and saw a young boy wind-surfing over the glittering blue water. He balanced himself confidently on the board, handling the sails smoothly as he skimmed along. "Oh, it looks like fun. Can we do that?"

"Yes, you can, but first you have to learn how to do it safely," Melanie promised. "That's what I meant by going to class. You begin by practicing on dry land."

"On dry land?" Benny wrinkled his nose. "I bet you don't get very far that way."

"No, that's true. But if you fall, you only

fall a few inches onto the sand." She reached down to ruffle Benny's hair. "We have a special wind-surfing simulator, Benny, and you feel just like you're on the water. It's a great way to practice."

"With none of the risks," Henry offered.

"Exactly." Melanie moved to the door. "Now if you boys want to get settled, I'll take the girls to their cabin."

A few minutes later, Soo Lee, Jessie, and Violet were unpacking their clothes in a spotless cabin almost identical to the boys'.

Jessie sat down cross-legged on her bed, studying a thick booklet. "Wow, have you seen this activity list? They have classes in everything you can think of — marine science, scuba diving, snorkeling, canoeing . . ."

"Oh, this looks good," Violet said, peering over her shoulder. "We can sign up to visit the site of an underwater shipwreck. Maybe we'll find some sunken treasure."

"I think that's for the advanced students

who know scuba diving," Jessie said. "We'll probably have to start with snorkeling and see how it goes." She started to say more, but a hearty knock at the door interrupted her.

"Hey, have you seen this!" Benny barreled into the room, waving the activity booklet. "Henry and I have already picked out our favorites," he announced. "Henry wants to learn underwater photography, and I want to learn ichy . . . ichy . . . how do you say this word?" He turned to his brother who was right behind him.

"Ichthyology," Henry told him.

"The study of fish," Jessie murmured.

"That's right," Benny said, bouncing on her bed. "I want to learn all about sharks." He thumbed eagerly through the book. "Everything in here looks good. We can swim over a coral reef, we can learn all about dolphins and whales. . . ." He scrunched his forehead in thought. "I don't know what to do first!"

"I think I can help you with that decision,"

Melanie said. The activity director was standing in the doorway, checking her watch. "In just three minutes, the bell is going to ring for dinner. How about if I walk you over to the dining hall?"

"Dinner?" Benny scrambled off the bed so fast he almost tumbled on the floor. "Let's go!"

Violet and Jessie laughed at the surprised look on Melanie's face.

"You just named his favorite activity of all," Jessie explained.

CHAPTER 2

A Night on the Water

"We have about thirty campers right now," Melanie explained as they moved through the cafeteria line. Benny had piled his plate high with spaghetti and meatballs and was reaching for a slice of Key lime pie. "Most of them are kids, but we have a few adult guests, too."

"I guess grown-ups like to learn about the ocean, just like we do," said Soo Lee thoughtfully.

"That's right." Melanie paused and

scanned the room. "You see that tall man with the beard sitting over by the window? That's Nick Simon. He's a marine biologist. That means he studies animals and plants that live in the ocean."

"Could we meet him?" Benny asked eagerly. "I have a zillion questions I'd like to ask him about fish."

"Sure," Melanie said, making her way past long tables filled with tanned campers in T-shirts and shorts, all enjoying delicious dinners. "Follow me."

A few minutes later, the Aldens were sitting down at a table with Nick Simon and a couple named Hilary and Joshua Slade, who ran a charter sailing company. Nick Simon was nice, but the Slades weren't very friendly. It seemed as if they'd rather be sitting alone.

A thin young woman approached the table. "Is there room for one more?" she asked. She spoke rapidly as if she were a little nervous.

"Of course, Katherine," Melanie said.

"We would be delighted if you'd join us."
She turned to the Aldens. "This is Katherine Kelly. She's an underwater photographer."

"That must be fun," Jessie said, biting into a piece of garlic bread.

Katherine Kelly shrugged. "Sometimes. I'm here to take some pictures of coral formations for an article in a nature magazine."

"I guess you know that we have a long stretch of coral here in the Keys," Melanie explained to the Aldens. "The reef runs a hundred and twenty-eight miles." She turned to Benny. "You'll get a chance to see some of it this week when we take a glass-bottom boat ride."

"Will I get to see all those fish I read about?" he asked Henry. Grandfather had bought Benny a book on tropical fish before they left home, and they had read some of it every night before bed.

"I'm sure you will see lots of them,"

Henry answered. "Which one is your favorite?"

"Oh, the car-wash fish," Benny said promptly.

"The car-wash fish?" Melanie laughed. "I've never heard of that one, and I've lived down here all my life."

"That's just a name I made up," Benny said. "It reminds me of a car wash. The fish all line up, and this really pretty blue fish cleans the tiny parasites off their bodies." He turned to Nick Simon. "What's the real name? I forget."

Nick Simon looked uncomfortable. "It's . . . well, that must be . . ." He scratched his chin, and looked helplessly at Melanie. "I can't seem to come up with the name of that fish."

"You must mean the blue angel fish," Melanie said slowly. Henry noticed that she looked a little taken aback. Nick Simon was a marine biologist. Surely he had heard of a blue angel fish?

"And I want to collect seashells," Benny announced. "Lots of them."

"Me too," Violet added. "I like the ones that are pink and white. You can hold them up to your ear."

"Oh, those are conch shells," Katherine Kelly said. "You'd better not touch them. You can get slapped with a five-hundred-dollar fine for removing them." She sounded annoyed.

"Five hundred dollars just for picking up a seashell?" Henry asked. He looked doubtful.

"She's right," Melanie assured him. "We have signs posted around Camp Coral to remind you. You're not allowed to take any conch shells from the camp." Her voice was very serious. "And you shouldn't even touch the coral because the bacteria on your hand can kill it."

"But my hands are clean!" Benny said. He held up his hands to show her, smiling proudly.

"I'm sure they are, Benny, but the slightest

human touch can destroy an entire stand of coral that took thousands of years to grow," Melanie insisted.

After dinner, the Aldens changed into bathing suits and joined Hilary and Joshua Slade and some other campers at the edge of the water. A boat was anchored at the shore, and Melanie was handing out plastic pails to everyone.

"What are we doing?" Soo Lee asked. "Are we going fishing?"

"Sort of. Each of you is going to collect specimens to keep in your aquarium. Just fill your pail with sea water, and step on the boat. I'll explain more once we get going," Melanie said.

"But I don't even have an aquarium," Benny protested.

"Oh, yes, you do." Melanie grinned. "You have your very own aquarium with your name on it in the ocean studies room. I checked it this morning. Each of you has one."

"My own aquarium!" Benny was excited. "What's in it?"

"Well, nothing but salt water just yet. But I bet you'll collect lots of exciting fish tonight."

Violet looked doubtful. "What if we pick the wrong fish?" she asked. "What if they eat each other?"

"Don't worry. I'll be here to help you." Melanie helped the campers into the boat. Then she cast off the thick rope that anchored it and signaled to a young man to start the engine.

They moved swiftly over the crystal water until Melanie signaled to stop the engine. "Let's stop. It's shallow here," she said, jumping overboard. The water rose just past her knees. "You can collect some really pretty sponges, and there are plenty of algae and sea fans."

"Ooh, there's something spiky down there," Violet said, peering nervously into the water.

"That's a sea urchin. You can take him. He'll do fine in your pail," Melanie assured her.

When everyone had gathered sponges and sea grass, they all got back in the pontoon boat and then headed for another shallow area.

"Oh, I see what I want," Soo Lee said as soon as the boat stopped. They were near the edge of a mangrove-lined shoreline. "It's a starfish!" she said, jumping into the water to collect her prize.

"I found a horseshoe crab," Henry said, plunging his hand underwater.

Benny had just used a net to capture a rainbow parrot fish when he noticed Joshua Slade grab something from the sandy sea bottom. He watched in amazement as the charter captain tucked it under his shirt. Was he really stuffing a fish inside his clothes? Why didn't he drop it in his bucket of salt water?

Before he could say anything, Violet an-

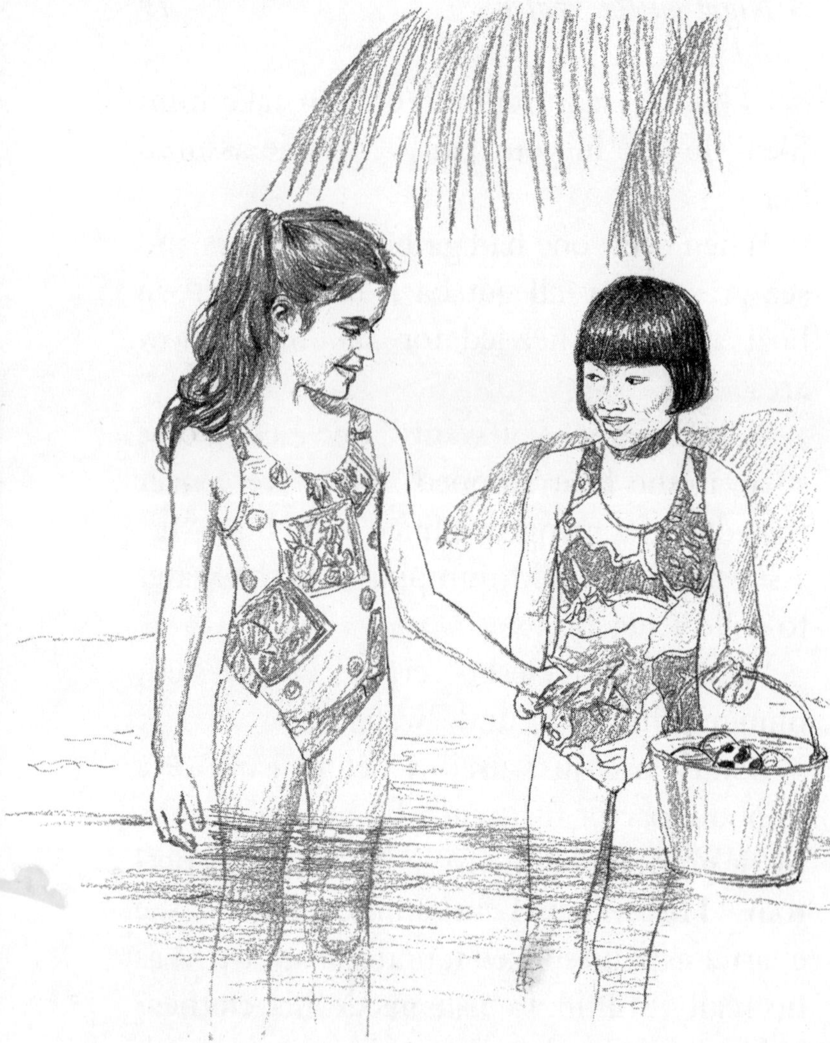

nounced that she had found a live conch, and with Melanie's permission, she placed it carefully in her pail.

"I thought we weren't allowed to take those," Hilary Slade objected.

"We return all the specimens to the ocean once we've studied them in the aquarium," Melanie reassured her. "This conch will never leave Camp Coral. It will go right back where it came from."

After the sun set, the group headed back to camp, where Melanie helped them set up their tanks. "You have a little free time now," Melanie said. "But I'd suggest you turn in early. We have a big day tomorrow."

"Your aquarium is beautiful," Soo Lee said a few minutes later. Violet had just arranged a sea fan against the rear wall of her five-gallon tank. Her prized conch was settled on a pile of red algae and sea grass.

"Thanks. Melanie said he eats algae, so I'm hoping he'll get hungry and come out."

"Did Melanie tell you what a conch looks like?" Henry asked her. "Like a big brown tongue!"

After everyone had finished arranging their tanks, they emptied their pails of sea water and stacked them neatly in the store-room. The Aldens left the classroom building and stepped into the balmy night air. There was a full moon, and a soft breeze rustled through the stately palms that fringed the grounds. A few of the staff members were building a fire on the beach, and someone was strumming a guitar.

"Do you want to join them on the beach?" Henry asked.

Benny gave an enormous yawn and Violet looked at Henry. "I think we should turn in. Benny looks like he's going to fall asleep standing up."

"I am not!" Benny said indignantly. He hated to go to bed because he never wanted to miss a moment's fun. He clapped his hand over his mouth just as he started to yawn again.

"Time to say good night," Henry said, steering his little brother toward the boys' cabin.

An hour later, Benny was tucked into bed, his mind filled with memories of the ride out to the grass flats. Collecting fish had been a lot of fun, and he was very proud of his beautiful parrot fish. Suddenly he frowned. He really should tell Henry about Joshua Slade hiding a fish inside his shirt! That was the strangest thing he had ever seen. Unless, of course, it wasn't a fish . . . but what else could it be? Before Benny could answer his own question, he drifted off to sleep.

Meanwhile, in the girls' cabin, Violet sat up in bed and whispered, "Soo Lee, are you awake?"

"I am now," Soo Lee answered with a laugh from the neighboring bed. "What's wrong?"

"I just remembered something. Did you notice if I turned on the filter in my aquarium?"

"I'm pretty sure that you did," Jessie said sleepily. "Didn't it make kind of a whooshing noise?"

"I don't know. I'm just not sure. If the filter isn't on, there won't be enough oxygen in the water." She bit her lip. "I don't know what to do."

"There's only one thing to do," Jessie said. "If you don't go back and check, you're going to worry about it all night."

"We'll come with you," Soo Lee offered. She reached for her robe.

Minutes later, the three girls made their way along the winding path to the classroom building. All the lights were out, but Violet was relieved to find the side door was unlocked. When Violet found the light switch, she hurried to the aquarium.

"See, I told you everything was okay," Jessie called to her. "I can see the water bubbling from here."

"Everything's not okay," Violet said in a trembly voice.

"What's wrong?" Jessie asked as she and Soo Lee hurried to Violet's side. Violet pointed wordlessly to her tank.

"Oh, no!" Soo Lee said. "Your beautiful conch shell is gone!"

CHAPTER 3

A Very Special Island

The next morning, Violet reported the theft to Melanie at breakfast. The counselor's expression was grim as she noted the time that the girls had visited the classroom building.

"Somebody really worked fast," she said. "I closed up half an hour earlier." She pushed her plate aside, her food untouched. "I must have forgotten to lock that side door, though," she said, shaking her head in disbelief.

"Why so glum? The scrambled eggs can't be that bad," Nick Simon joked, sliding into the seat next to her. He had a plate of pancakes and a steaming cup of coffee.

"Somebody stole Violet's conch shell," Benny said. "They took it right out of her aquarium last night."

"Really?" Nick's eyes darkened.

"I'll have to report it to the authorities," Melanie said quietly. "Nothing like this has ever happened before."

Jessie looked around the crowded cafeteria. It was hard to believe, but the person who stole the conch shell could be eating breakfast in the dining hall at that very moment!

Melanie noticed Violet's downcast expression. "How about if I take all of you on an outing this morning? I can't promise you another conch shell, but I'll show you a beautiful spot."

Violet brightened. "Where are we going?" she asked.

"To my own hidden beach." Melanie lowered her voice. "It's a very special place and no one else knows about it."

"You own your own beach?" Soo Lee asked.

"Not exactly." Melanie smiled. "But when I'm all alone there, sitting under a palm tree, I can pretend that I do! It's my favorite place to be."

Half an hour later, the Aldens were skimming over the water in a small powerboat. The water shimmered in the bright sunlight as Melanie maneuvered the craft toward a tiny island.

"We're going to an island!" Benny exclaimed.

"There are hundreds of islands in the Keys," Melanie explained. "A lot of them don't even have names. I discovered this one a few years ago. And ever since, it's been my special place."

When they reached the island, Melanie cut the motor and pointed to a dense thicket of mangrove trees. "I'm afraid we have to take

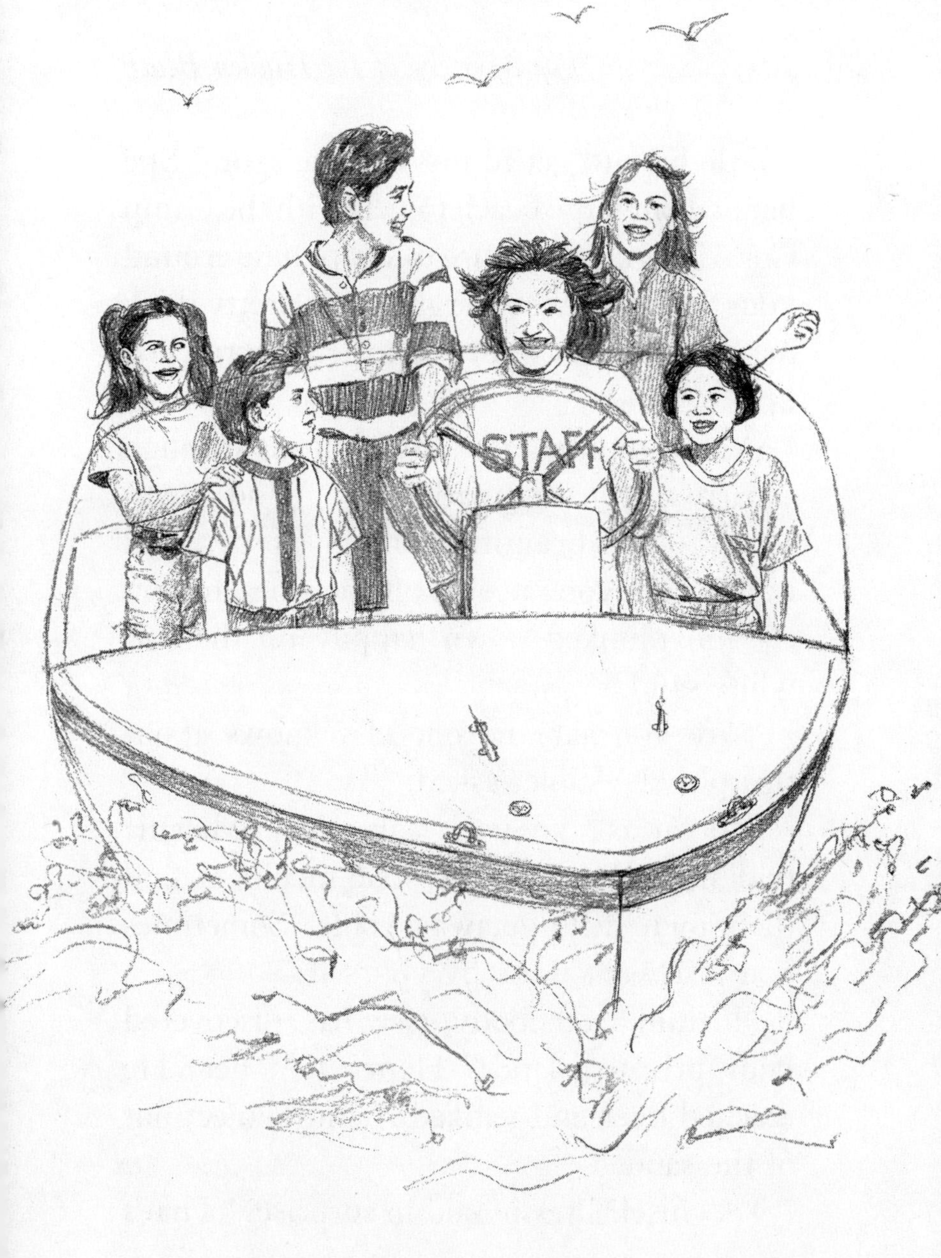
STAFF

a little hike to get to my favorite spot." She handed out large beach towels with the Camp Coral insignia. "Be sure to wrap these around your waists. The undergrowth is pretty thick here, and I don't want you to get all scratched up."

A few minutes later, after cutting through a narrow, twisting path, they found themselves on a beautiful stretch of deserted beach. Everyone peeled off their beach towels and plunked down happily on the soft white sand.

"Are you sure no one else knows about this place?" Violet asked.

"As far as I know, it's all mine," Melanie told her. "Most of the staff members find their own little getaway spots. Sometimes you just want to be by yourself."

"I think somebody else has discovered your private island," Henry told her. He reached over and yanked a shiny object out of the sand.

"A chisel?" Jessie said in surprise. "That's

strange. Why would anyone bring a chisel to the beach?"

Melanie shook her head. "I can't imagine." She looked at the bright yellow handle. "It's not from Camp Coral. We stamp all our tools with a double C."

"Melanie, can we go swimming?" Benny asked. The bright Florida sun was making him hot.

"Sure, or how about wading? There's a really nice coral bed here and we can take a few pictures, if you like." Melanie reached into her duffel bag and pulled out a small camera and some goggles. "Who wants to be the photographer?"

"I do." Violet said, jumping to her feet."I've never seen an underwater camera before."

"I'll show you how to use it. It's really easy," Melanie told her.

Everyone waded out into the warm water, and Melanie led them to a patch of brightly colored coral.

"I thought you had to go way out in the ocean to find coral," Henry said.

Melanie nodded. "To get to the barrier reef, you do. That's where we're going tomorrow. But this kind of coral — shallow bay coral — is found in knee-deep water." She handed Violet the camera and quickly explained how to use it.

"Remember, don't touch anything," Jessie said to Benny. He was staring at a clump of coral just a foot away.

Melanie handed out goggles to everyone. "You really have to put your face in the water to get the full effect of the colors. Take a look. That's golf ball coral right next to your foot. And there's a nice chunk of finger coral over on the right."

"Something strange is going on down here," Violet said, startled. She pulled her head out of the water, still clutching the camera. "I tried to get a picture of some coral and it moved!"

Melanie peered into the clear blue water. "Oh, that's rose coral, Violet. Whenever it gets covered up with sand, it spits out a little jet of water. That's how it turns itself right side up."

They waded around for another half hour, being careful not to disturb the coral in any way. Violet took a lot of pictures, and Benny was excited when he spotted a strange-looking fish swimming past him.

"Hey!" he yelled to Melanie. "What's that?" He pointed to a small translucent disk bobbing on the water.

"A jellyfish," she replied.

"Are you sure it's a fish? It's got something green trapped inside it," Jessie said. "It looks like a plant."

"It is a plant. Some jellyfish carry their food with them," Melanie explained.

"Just like we put granola bars in our back-packs," Benny piped up.

"Exactly."

After they'd eaten a tasty lunch, Melanie took the Aldens back to camp. There they piled into a van with some other campers to visit Key West.

Jessie admired the beautiful old Victorian houses, with tropical plants spilling out of their window boxes. The streets were lined with stately palms and banyan trees, and the air smelled like flowers.

They drove toward Mallory Square on a street lined with shops. A vendor was cutting open fresh coconuts and selling them to a group of children, who raised the rough brown shells to their lips.

"What are they doing?" Violet asked, puzzled.

"They're sipping fresh coconut milk," Melanie told her. "It's delicious. If we have time, we'll stop and buy some on the way back."

After Melanie parked the van, they wandered through an open air market that was filled with tourists. The hot afternoon sun made everyone move slowly. Violet watched as a man made a basket out of palm fronds. Soo Lee bought a delicate bracelet with the money Grandfather had given each of them for souvenirs. Benny looked over a selection of shells, and finally chose a chalky white sand dollar.

After Benny paid for his prize, he looked up in surprise. "Look, there's Nick Simon from camp." He pointed to a tall bearded man who was deep in conversation with another man. "I want to show him my new sand dollar."

Melanie watched as Benny scampered over to the marine biologist. "That's funny," she said.

"What's that?" Jessie was picking through a pile of tiny brass rings.

"I asked Nick Simon if he'd like to ride into Key West with us today, but he told me he had too much to do back at camp," she said with a shrug. "I guess he changed his mind."

"Nick Simon liked my sand dollar!" Benny said, running back to the group. "And guess what — he told me his friend is a real fisherman!"

Henry glanced over at Nick Simon's friend, a pale, sandy-haired man in his early thirties. The two men quickly turned their backs and headed down to the docks. "He sure doesn't look like a fisherman," Henry said. "Look how pale he is. He looks like he never goes in the sun."

"Everybody else around here is tan," Jessie said. She shrugged. "Maybe he's the captain of the fishing boat, and he stays inside while other people fish."

"Maybe," Melanie said, but she didn't look convinced.

"Where shall we go now?" Violet asked. She sat under a date tree and unfolded her Key West map. "We can go to the Key West Aquarium, or we can see Mel Fisher's Museum."

"What kind of museum is it?" Benny was peering over her shoulder.

"It has all kinds of sunken treasure," Melanie explained. "Mel Fisher discovered the *Atocha*, a ship that sank hundreds of years ago. It was filled with gold bars, and lots of emeralds and jewelry."

"But the aquarium is interesting, too," Violet pointed out. "It has loads of fish, Benny, and I've heard they even let you touch an eel."

"Wow!" Benny exclaimed. He was stumped. Fish or sunken treasure — how could he ever choose? He turned to Melanie. "Could we do both?" he asked. "We could go to the aquarium right now and then come back to Key West another day to visit the museum."

"That's fine with me," Melanie said with a smile. "I can see that you don't want to miss anything."

Jessie laughed as Benny hopped up and down. No one had more energy than her little brother!

CHAPTER 4

Petting a Shark

"So that's why they call them parrot fish!" Violet said excitedly a few minutes later. Melanie and the Aldens were peering into a large tank at the Key West Aquarium where a dazzling fish zipped through the crystal-clear water. It was brightly colored and had a beak almost like a bird's.

"Parrot fish use their beaks to scrape algae off the coral," Melanie explained. "Unfortunately, they can leave some pretty bad scars on the reef."

Jessie steered them to another large tank, where a young man was giving a lecture. He lifted something dark and wriggly out of the tank, and held it up carefully in front of the visitors. "This is a nurse shark," the man explained. "Would anyone here like to pet her?"

Benny's eyes lit up. "Can I?" When the man nodded, Benny stepped closer and carefully stroked the shark's side. Then he drew his hand back in surprise. "It feels just like sandpaper!"

"Will it bite?" Violet asked, waiting her turn to touch the shark.

"No, nurse sharks are completely harmless. They're very gentle," Melanie told the Aldens."

After they learned about porcupine puffers and sea cucumbers, the guide lifted a large conch shell out of the tank.

"That's just like the one you found," Jessie whispered to Violet.

"I know," Violet said, admiring the pink and white spiral shell. She wondered who had broken into the classroom building that night, and if the thief would ever be caught. She hoped so.

"This is the horse conch," the guide was saying. "Maybe he'll come out for us." He waited until something large and brown slithered out of the shell.

"There he is!" Benny leaned forward for a closer look.

Everyone watched as the conch inched across the guide's hand, and then lumbered slowly back into his shell. "The conch is a very interesting marine animal. He eats red algae and moves one mile in twenty-four hours."

"Wow! That's pretty slow," Henry pointed out.

Benny giggled. "Not if you're carrying your house on your back!" He suddenly spied a pretty blue fish in another tank. "Look," he said, tugging at Melanie's hand.

"That's the fish I told you about. The car-wash fish."

Melanie nodded. "The blue angel fish," she said, reading the label on the tank. "You have a good memory, Benny," she told him. "He cleans up the other fish by eating parasites off them."

The same fish that Nick Simon had never heard of, Henry thought.

Later that night over a delicious dinner of fried chicken and mashed potatoes, Benny was telling the whole table about his visit to the aquarium.

"We even saw a barracuda," he said proudly. "He was swimming really fast underwater."

Nick Simon smiled at him politely. "They can be very dangerous," he pointed out. "Just remember to get out of the water if you see one headed your way," he added jokingly.

"Or better yet, don't wear any jewelry while you're swimming." Melanie said,

ing to a thin silver chain around Nick Simon's neck.

The marine biologist looked at her blankly. It was clear to everyone that he had no idea what she was talking about. Violet finally turned to Melanie. "What do you mean?"

Melanie shrugged. "Everyone knows that barracuda are attracted to things that are shiny. If they see a flash of silver in the water — like a chain — they think it's something to eat. You see, their favorite food is a type of little silvery fish." She paused and stared right at Nick Simon. "But then, you know that."

"Yes, of course," Nick said quickly. He looked a little embarrassed.

"I definitely don't want to be dinner for a fish!" Benny exclaimed and everyone laughed.

"Don't worry, Benny," Melanie reassured him. "We'll make sure that you're not."

When dinner was over, the Aldens decided to check on their aquariums. Jessie had picked up a few pretty, colorful shells at the market and she wanted to add them to the tank.

They were working in the classroom building, when suddenly Benny remembered something. He tugged at Henry's wrist. "Something really strange happened the night we went out in the pontoon boat." He quickly told everyone about seeing Joshua Slade pluck something out of the ocean and hide it in his shirt.

"He didn't put it into his bucket the way he was supposed to," Benny said, confused. "He stuffed it right here." He pointed to his chest.

"What was it?" Soo Lee asked.

"It couldn't have been a live fish," Jessie pointed out, sensibly. "It would have been wriggling."

"Maybe it was a conch shell," Violet offered, thinking of her own shell.

"No, that would be too big to fit under his shirt," Henry said.

"Maybe it was a really pretty shell and he didn't want the rest of us to see it." Jessie

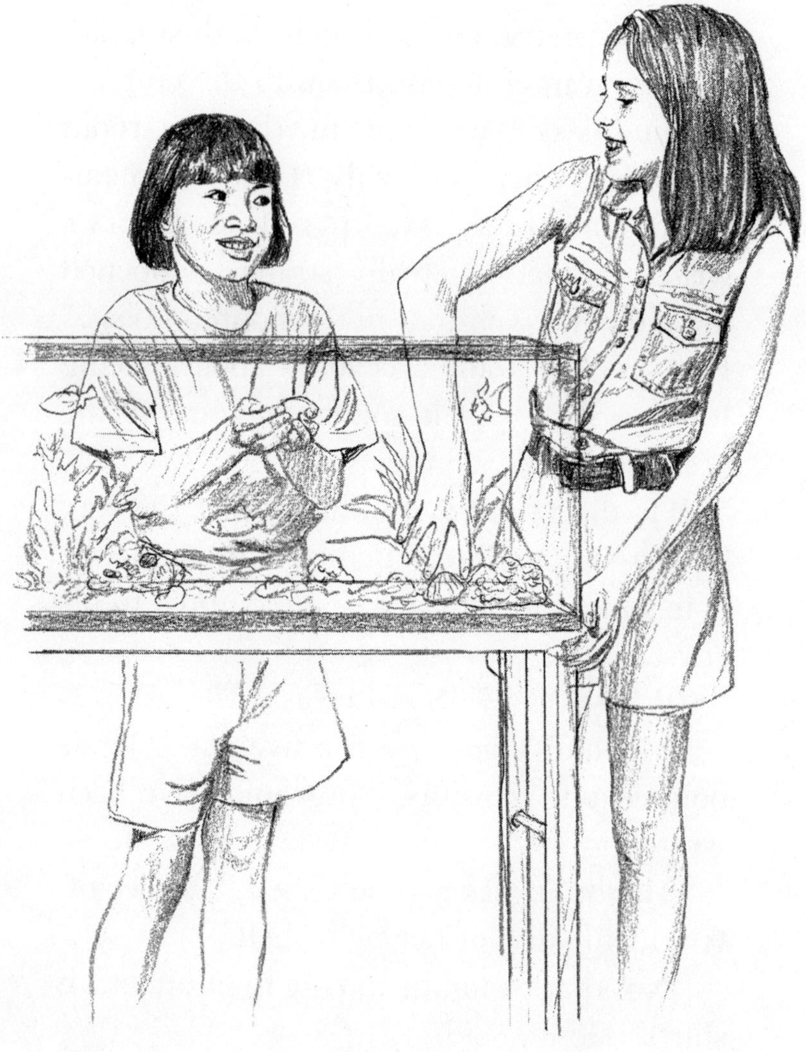

suggested as she carefully added a sea fan to her tank.

"But what did he do with it?" Soo Lee asked. She glanced at the tank that Joshua Slade shared with his wife. It was almost empty except for a few wisps of sea grass and a couple of angel fish. "He didn't put it in his tank."

On the way back to their cabins, they noticed Ned, one of the counselors, guiding a boat toward the dock. The craft was filled with campers, and Violet remembered that a night expedition was scheduled that evening. Usually boats weren't taken out at night, but this was a special occasion.

"Let's see what they got," Benny said eagerly. "Melanie said you can find some nice fish that only come out at night."

They were almost at the water's edge when they spotted Joshua Slade strolling by. He seemed lost in thought and was startled when Ned tossed him a line from the boat. "Would you mind tying that for us?" Ned asked.

"Sure, I . . . I'll be glad to." Joshua Slade

looked helplessly at the line in his hand, and looped it uncertainly around the piling. "There you go," he said brightly, and hurried off.

When Ned leaped nimbly off the boat, he looked at the line and shook his head. "What kind of knot is this?" Henry heard him mutter. "The guy doesn't know how to tie up a boat!"

"Did you hear that?" Henry asked as soon as they were out of earshot. They were walking down the winding path that led to the cabins.

Jessie nodded. "Mr. Slade is supposed to run a sailing company, but he doesn't know how to tie a knot?" She paused. "That doesn't make any sense at all."

"A lot of things don't make sense," Violet added. "Mr. Simon is supposed to be a marine biologist, but he didn't know that barracuda like to eat little silvery fish. Melanie had to explain it to him."

"And he didn't know about the car-wash fish," Benny reminded her.

"That's right," Henry agreed. "And now look at Mr. Slade. I never heard of a sailor who couldn't tie a simple knot!"

They were at the girls' cabin, and Violet stopped outside the door. "I'm beginning to think that Melanie is the only person around here who really knows everything she's supposed to."

"She sure does," Benny said enthusiastically. "I like her a lot!"

"We all do," Jessie said. "Time to turn in, little brother. We have a big day tomorrow."

"I know," Benny said, dancing down the path to the boys' cabin excitedly. "Windsurfing at eight, sailing at ten, and snorkeling at two."

"Aren't you forgetting something?" Henry said teasingly.

Benny thought a moment, then shook his head. "I don't think so."

"Breakfast at seven!"

Benny grinned and rubbed his stomach. "I could never forget that!"

* * *

The next morning, Benny raced through the cafeteria line so he could be the first one to try the wind-surfing simulator. It was a wide flat board, mounted on a giant spring. If you stepped on the board and shifted your weight, you felt just like you were bouncing back and forth over the waves. "It seems funny surfing on dry land," he said, as he hopped on the machine.

"You won't think it's so funny if you land on your bottom," Melanie told him. "The beach sand is nice and cushiony. It will break your fall."

"I won't fall," Benny said.

"Maybe not." Melanie positioned his feet on the board. "But nine out of ten people do. It's a lot harder than it looks."

For the next ten minutes, Benny practiced balancing on the board and working the sails. "Wow, this is hard," he said, tugging the sail in one direction, then another. "But it must be lots of fun when you finally try it in the ocean."

"It's a lot of fun," Melanie promised. "But we have to make sure you do it safely on land first. And once you're on the water, you'll be wearing a life jacket. That's in case you tumble into the water," she said. "Not that I think you will."

Each of the Aldens took turns, and Jessie caught the hang of it right away. "When can we try the real thing?" she asked, her face flushed with excitement.

"I know you think you're ready to go right now, but you still need some more practice," Melanie said firmly. "I want everybody out here for half an hour every day, because you can't try it in the ocean until you master it on land."

"Oh no!" Benny groaned.

"It's not easy," Melanie pointed out. "But if you practice hard, we'll try to get you on the water, Benny."

CHAPTER 5

Someone's Stealing Coral!

The following afternoon, Melanie invited the Aldens back to her favorite beach for a delicious picnic lunch. They had spent the morning learning all about dolphins.

"I asked the cook to pack some special lunches for us," she said, pointing to a large cooler. "Sandwiches, fruit, and fresh lemonade." She looked at Benny. "Plus a dozen homemade brownies," she said, knowing his eyes would light up.

"Let's go!" Benny said, racing down to the dock.

"What did you learn about dolphins this morning?" Melanie asked half an hour later. They were sprawled on beach towels, enjoying their lunch.

"Our teacher said they're really smart," Benny said. "They talk to each other with special sounds, and they like to play." He paused, munching on his sandwich. "And they love to eat. They eat about twenty pounds of fish a day!"

Violet laughed. "I guess you've finally met your match, Benny."

"Dolphins always look happy," Soo Lee added. "It looks like they are smiling."

"But they only look that way because their mouths turn up at the corners," Henry said. "The instructor told us that they get bored and unhappy sometimes, just like people. That's why it's not fair to keep them caged up in little pools to do tricks. They enjoy living with other dolphins in the ocean."

After lunch, Melanie and Henry wandered down to the water's edge. Melanie scuffed her toe on a seashell and looked down in surprise. "That's funny. It looks like someone else has been here." She stared at a set of footprints in the hard-packed sand along the shoreline.

Soo Lee ran across the beach to join them. "Can I wade out and look at the coral?" she asked.

"Sure," Melanie said good-naturedly. She looked worried, though, and Henry knew she was upset that someone had been on her island.

Henry and Melanie were ambling along the shore when a sudden shout from Soo Lee made them turn in alarm.

"What's wrong?" Henry shaded his eyes from the bright sun.

"It's gone!" Soo Lee said, peering into the water. "The coral!"

"Oh no," Melanie said, dropping to her knees in the shallow water. "It looks like someone's taken a sledge hammer to it!"

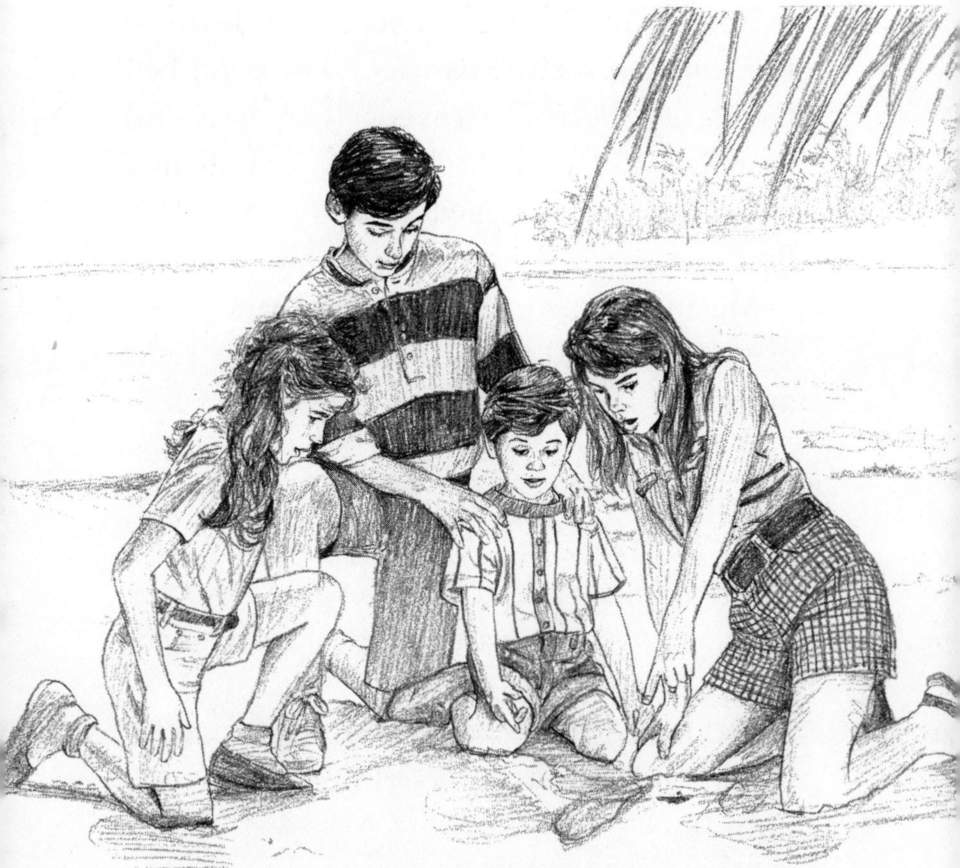

Benny, Jessie, and Violet raced down to the water to see the damage. The coral bed had truly been destroyed. The beautiful branches had been hacked off, and all that remained was a jagged base on the ocean floor.

Melanie turned to them with tears in her eyes. "We need to go back to camp right away and report this."

"Of course," Jessie said. The children helped Melanie gather up the picnic things. They hurried back to the powerboat and Melanie quickly started the engine. As they skimmed over the water, everyone was silent except Benny.

"I don't understand," he said. "Why would anyone want to ruin anything so beautiful?"

"For money." Melanie's voice was tight as she steered the boat skillfully over the gentle, lapping waves. "Coral is worth a fortune, and there's not much of it left."

"But how did anyone even know about that particular coral bed?" Henry asked.

"You said you've been coming to the island for years, and it's always been deserted."

"I don't know," Melanie admitted. "But that's something I need to tell the Coast Guard."

"The Coast Guard?" Benny's eyes were wide.

"Stealing coral is a serious crime," Melanie told him. "We'll call the authorities as soon as we hit camp. I bet they'll start an investigation right away."

An hour later, the Aldens found themselves being interviewed by Mr. Larson, a friendly man from the local Coast Guard Station.

"Can you describe the coral bed?" he asked the children. "I already have Melanie's statement, but you might have something to add."

"It was a very large bed, and really pretty," Jessie began. "I know there was rose coral and finger coral, because Melanie pointed it out to us. . . ."

"Wait a minute!" Violet blurted out. "We can do more than describe it — we can show you a picture of it!" She turned to Melanie. "Remember, you showed me how to use that underwater camera."

"So I did," Melanie said, looking relieved. "Now we'll have an exact record of the bed."

"Where's your camera?" Mr. Larson asked.

"It's in my cabin," Melanie said. "I can get it for you."

"Did someone mention pictures?" Katherine Kelly asked. She had walked into the lodge so quietly no one had heard her. "Maybe I can help. I'm an underwater photographer."

"I don't think so, Katherine," Melanie said. She looked at Mr. Larson to see if he would volunteer any information, but he shook his head very slightly. Apparently he wasn't ready to discuss the case with anyone else just yet.

Katherine Kelly waited awkwardly for a

moment, and then said brusquely, "Well, I'd better get going then. I've got a lot of work to do this afternoon."

As she turned to leave, Benny noticed a series of thin red scratches on Katherine Kelly's calves. "What happened to your legs?" he blurted out.

The photographer glanced down in embarrassment. "Oh, it's nothing," she said, touching the fiery red marks. "I was playing with Horace, and I guess he got carried away." She managed a thin smile before hurrying from the room.

"Horace?" Violet said in amazement. She had met the large orange tabby when they had first arrived at camp. "He's the world's friendliest cat. He never scratches anyone."

"Not even Bingo the dog," Benny piped up.

On her way back with the camera for Mr. Larson, Violet bumped into Joshua Slade.

"Taking some pictures?" he asked.

Violet nodded. "I have a roll ready to be developed."

"What did you photograph?" He seemed unusually talkative, and Violet wondered why he was so interested.

"Some tropical fish, some pretty sea grass. . . ." She thought it was better not to mention the coral or the ongoing investigation.

"Oh, is that all . . . see you later!" Joshua walked abruptly away.

What did he mean by that? Violet wondered. What had he thought she was going to say?

After Violet handed over the film to Mr. Larson, she and Melanie strolled back to the beach to practice wind-surfing. The rest of the Aldens had decided to spend the afternoon learning about underwater shipwrecks. "I know you feel really sad about the coral bed," Violet said.

"I do," Melanie admitted. "It was very special to me." She bent down to adjust the wind-surfer. "I just hope they find the thief before any more coral is lost. It takes thousands of years to grow, and it can never be replaced."

She helped Violet position her feet on the small board, and showed her how to move the sails. "Do you remember what I taught you?"

"I think so." Violet kept her balance and tugged at the sails, just as if she were on the ocean. But her mind was elsewhere. Joshua Slade was friendly one minute, and unfriendly the next. Why? Katherine Kelly was covered with scratches and blamed it on the cat. But the cat was friendly and never scratched anyone. And Nick Simon didn't seem to know a thing about marine biology. There were so many mysteries at Camp Coral.

"Violet, hold the sails with more force. You're letting them get too slack!" Melanie said.

"Sorry," Violet muttered and tightened her grip.

"That's much better," Melanie said approvingly. "You'll be out in the waves in no time."

"Thanks." Violet smiled at the counselor, still thinking. None of the little mysteries could compare to the big mystery they were all facing. Who was stealing coral? Violet would have some free time after dinner that evening, and she knew exactly how she was going to spend it. It was time for an Alden family conference. Maybe all four of them — and Soo Lee, of course — could catch the thief and solve the mystery.

CHAPTER 6

Benny Finds an Unusual Coin

The camp was quiet when the Aldens gathered at a picnic table down by the dock later that evening. Many of the campers used their free time to read and relax in their cabins, while others worked on their craft projects like painting, macrame and pottery.

Violet told everyone her suspicions of Katherine Kelly, Joshua Slade, and Nick Simon. When she finished, no one said anything for a moment.

"Does anyone have any ideas?" she asked, watching as Benny skimmed a flat rock over the water.

Henry looked thoughtful. "I wonder if there could be a logical explanation for some of the things we've noticed."

"There's something else funny about Joshua Slade," Benny said. "Remember, I saw him stuff a fish in his shirt."

Jessie laughed. "We're not sure it was a fish, Benny, but you're right," she said. "It sounds like he was hiding something that day we were all out collecting specimens together."

"That's true," Soo Lee agreed. "But what about Katherine Kelly? I can't believe that Horace really scratched her legs."

"You're right, that does seem strange," Jessie offered. "But why would she lie about it?" Suddenly she remembered the first day they had visited Melanie's island. They had wrapped beach towels around their legs to protect themselves from the dense underbrush. "The mangrove trees!" she exclaimed.

"If Katherine Kelly scratched her legs when she was stealing coral on Melanie's island, she wouldn't want anyone to know about it. She had to explain the scratches somehow, so she blamed Horace."

"But how would she get to the island?" Henry asked. "Only counselors are allowed to use the boats."

"She could go out very quietly at night when everyone was asleep," Soo Lee suggested.

"I saw lights on the water one night!" Benny said, turning back to the group. "Do you think that's a clue?"

Jessie smiled. Benny always loved to solve a mystery. "There are probably a lot of boats on the water at night, Benny, and they all have lights." When she saw the disappointed look on his face, she added, "That could be a good clue, though, Benny. We'll have to remember that."

Henry was leaning against a palm tree, staring out at the darkening sky. "You know, I just thought of something else important.

Remember that chisel I found the first day at the island? That could have been left there by the thief."

"That's a good point," Jessie said. "We need to mention that to Mr. Larson from the Coast Guard. I'm sure he'll be back tomorrow — "

Suddenly a slim figure stepped out from the shadows. "A lovely evening, isn't it?" Hilary Slade smiled at Benny and skimmed a stone across the water, just as he had done a few minutes earlier. "I used to love to do this, too, when I was a kid," she said in a friendly way.

Had she been standing there all the time? Violet wondered. Had she been eavesdropping on their conversation?

Henry was puzzled too. Why was she making such an effort to be nice? She rarely bothered to talk to the children at dinner and had only spoken a few words to them during their whole time at camp.

Hilary turned her attention to Soo Lee. "That's beautiful," she said, touching the bright yellow jute. "It's macrame, isn't it? How did you ever learn to do that?"

"I'm taking a craft class," Soo Lee explained. "It's not very hard," she added, holding up the bright yellow band. "I picked an easy pattern. It has only two different kinds of knots."

"Two kinds of knots?" Hilary looked impressed. "I could never do that. I'm all thumbs."

"No, it's easy, really," Soo Lee insisted. She handed her the strip of macrame. "All you have to know is a square knot and a half-hitch." She pronounced these new words carefully.

"Never heard of them," Hilary said with a laugh. "I guess I'll take your word for it, though."

Soo Lee looked surprised. "But my teacher said they are the same knots sailors use." she said. "Don't you use them on your boats?"

"Oh, well . . ." Hilary's face was flushed

and she looked embarrassed. "I leave all that up to my husband." She quickly thrust the macrame into Soo Lee's hands. "Well," she said briskly, "look how dark the sky is getting. I must be getting back to the cabin. See you tomorrow!" Before anyone could say a word, she turned away and hurried down the path.

"She certainly wanted to leave in a hurry," Violet said.

"I think she didn't want us to know that she didn't recognize those sailing knots," Jessie added.

"So now there are four people who are suspects," Soo Lee said.

"Four?" Benny asked. "I thought we had three — Joshua and Hilary Slade, and Katherine Kelly."

"Don't forget about Nick Simon," Henry said grimly. "Every time anyone asks him a question about fish, he seems to draw a blank."

"And he's supposed to be a marine biologist!" Jessie exclaimed.

"And there's something else about him," Henry said. "He seemed worried when we spotted him in Key West talking to that fisherman friend of his."

"Who might not be a fisherman at all." Jessie stood up. "Remember how pale he was?"

Henry nodded. "I don't think he's telling the truth about his friend, but I can't imagine why he would lie."

Benny yawned, and Jessie took him by the hand. "I think we should all get a good night's sleep, and maybe we can figure out some answers tomorrow."

When Benny started to get up, he noticed an old coin wedged between the wooden slats of the picnic table.

"Look!" said Benny, showing the coin to Henry and Jessie. "I'm going to keep this!" The coin was dented and uneven around the edges, but Benny didn't mind. He loved to collect things, and he stuck it in his pocket.

The next morning at breakfast, the Aldens sat at a long table by the window, discussing the mystery. They stopped talking abruptly

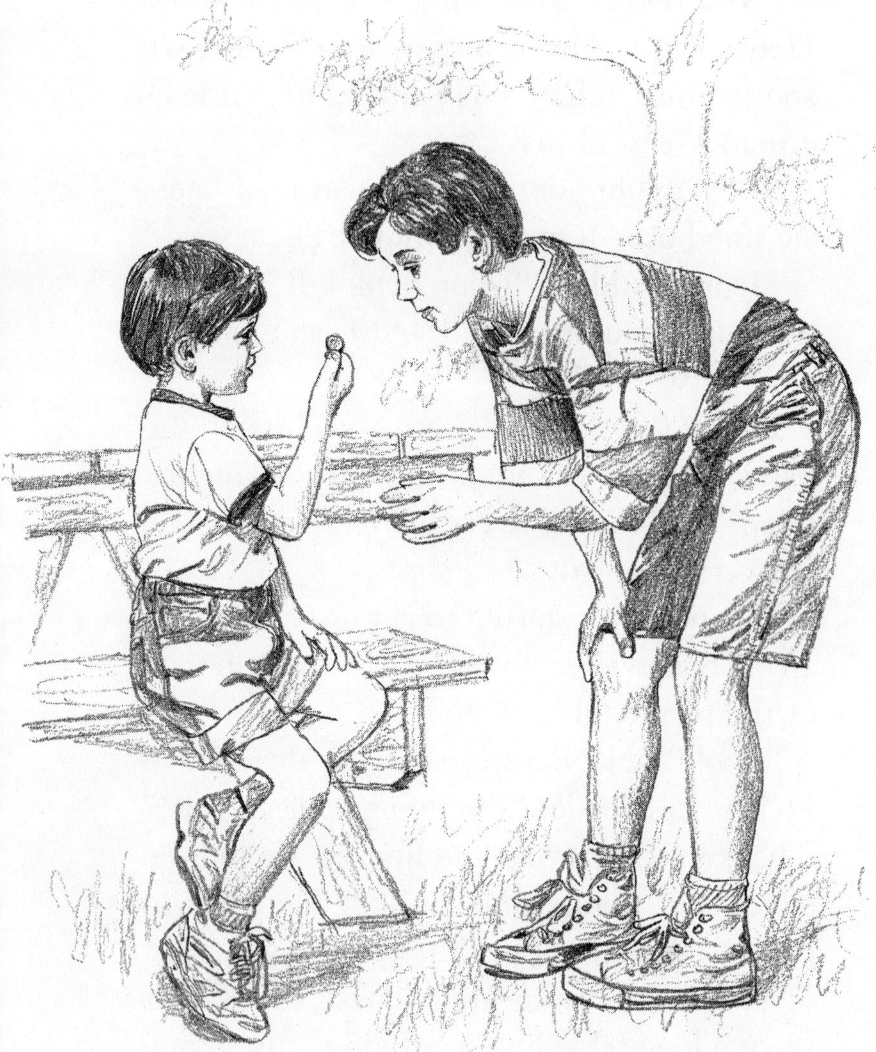

when Joshua and Hilary Slade joined them.

"Good morning!" Hilary said cheerily to the Aldens.

Everyone greeted her politely, but Henry was more suspicious than ever. Why was she being so friendly?

"What are your plans for the day?" Joshua asked.

"We're going on a glass-bottom boat ride over the coral reef this morning," Jessie told him. "And then we're going back to Key West in the afternoon to visit a treasure museum."

"A treasure museum! That certainly sounds like fun," Hilary said. "Wouldn't it be just wonderful to find some real buried treasure?"

"That's what Mel Fisher did," Henry told her. "He and his wife discovered a famous ship called the *Atocha*. It was a Spanish galleon that went down in a hurricane in the 1600's off the coast of Florida."

"I read about it," Jessie said. "It had been lying on the ocean floor all that time, and was full of treasure — gold bars, coins, and jewels. People had been looking for it for years, but it was Mel Fisher who finally found it."

"Did he bring it up?" Benny asked excitedly. "Can we go see it?"

"The *Atocha* is still on the ocean floor, but he brought up all the treasure. He has a lot of it on display in his museum," Henry told his brother.

"And that's where we're going today!" Benny said. "Yippee!"

"You seem to be really interested in treasure," Joshua said.

"I am! I collect coins," Benny said proudly. "I found a really interesting one last night."

"Really? What's it like?" Joshua stopped eating, his fork in midair.

"Well, it's really old, and it's hard to read what it says on it." He paused, surprised at their interest.

"Do you have it with you?" Hilary asked sharply.

"No, it's back in my room." Benny looked a little uncertain. Hilary suddenly seemed irritated with him.

"What else did you notice about the coin?" her husband persisted.

Benny shrugged. "It's uneven around the edges." He grinned. "That's what I like about it. That's what makes it special."

"Does it have any markings on it?" Hilary leaned close to him, her eyes piercing. "Try to remember."

Benny scrunched his forehead in thought.

"It has a coat of arms on it, doesn't it?" Violet said.

"A coat of arms!" Hilary was so excited she jiggled her cup, and her coffee flooded the saucer. She pushed it away and looked at her husband. "I don't feel very hungry. Why don't we head back to the cabin?"

"Good idea." Joshua pushed back his chair. "See you later," he said briefly to the children.

"Those two are acting really suspicious lately," Jessie said quietly to the others. "I think we should keep an eye on them."

Jessie nodded and swallowed a forkful of pancakes. "So do I. Right now, there are four suspects, and the Slades are at the top of the list."

CHAPTER 7

A Trip to the Coral Reef

"You're going to see some beautiful coral out at the reef," Melanie said, as they boarded a glass-bottom boat later that morning. They had driven into Key West after breakfast and were taking their seats on the upper deck of a large white boat called the *Fury*.

"And fish, too?" Benny asked. He had already learned to identify several kinds of tropical fish, and wanted to see more.

Melanie laughed. "Over six hundred varieties. That's enough to satisfy any fish lover!"

As soon as the boat got under way, Melanie asked the children what they knew about the coral reef.

"I know it's over a hundred miles long," Violet said. "And it runs just offshore of the Florida Keys."

"That's right," Melanie agreed.

"Why don't we have any coral reefs up near Greenfield?" Benny asked.

"Because the reef is made up of coral polyps, and they need warm water to survive. They die if you put them in water that's cooler than seventy degrees."

An hour later, they dropped anchor over a large coral bed, and everyone went below to the observation deck. "Wow, now I see why they call this a glass-bottom boat!" Benny dashed along the narrow walkways dividing glass panels that revealed the ocean floor.

"The fish are so close we could touch

them," Violet said, watching as a midnight-blue parrot fish glided by.

"I think this fish had too much to eat," Benny said, dropping to his knees to get a better look. He pointed to a large tan fish that looked almost round.

"That's a Southern puffer," Melanie said. "He's not really fat, Benny. He sucks in a bellyfull of water and makes himself look three times as big. That way, he scares off other fish who might bother him."

Jessie admired some beautiful elkhorn, staghorn, and branch coral, and Melanie reminded her that they grow only two or three inches a year.

"It's seems funny that coral is actually alive," Violet pointed out.

"But it's true. The coral reef is constantly growing new colonies of polyps on top of the skeletons of older ones. Coral can live for centuries. The reef is thousands of years old."

As Melanie talked about the reef, Henry's

mind went back to the coral theft on the island. Would the Coast Guard be able to catch the thief? he wondered. He went over the list of suspects that they had come up with, and felt confused. That was the whole problem, he decided. There were plenty of suspects, but no real clues. And worst of all, no proof!

After lunch, the group headed to the Mel Fisher Museum to see the riches of the famous Spanish ship, the *Atocha*. Benny was thrilled to touch a genuine gold bar, and Jessie admired a beautiful belt studded with rubies and diamonds. "Do you know dolphins were trained to bring up some of the emeralds from the wreck?" a museum guide asked.

"Emeralds? Why would dolphins be interested in emeralds?" Violet asked, puzzled.

"Because we rewarded them with their favorite treat — mackerel!"   ·

* * *

That evening, at bedtime, Benny thought about his own treasure — the bent coin he had found at the dock. He had seen a picture of Mel Fisher wearing a gold coin on a chain around his neck. Benny wanted to do the same thing. "Henry, can you drill a hole in my coin tomorrow?"

"Sure, Benny, I'll be glad to." Henry tucked the covers around his little brother, and within minutes, both boys fell fast asleep.

It was nearly midnight when Benny awoke with a start. He heard a faint rustling noise, but he couldn't pinpoint exactly where it was coming from. And he was too scared to open his eyes.

"Henry, is that you?" he whispered. There was no answer. He strained to listen, as goosebumps rose on his arms. Should he scramble out of bed and wake his brother? He decided to wait a couple of more minutes.

He was completely awake now, and he knew he wasn't imagining what he heard.

Something was brushing against the lampshade on his night table. Something was jiggling the brush and comb on his dresser top. Something was bumping into his bed.

"Henry?" Benny said softly, his voice trembling.

Just then he heard the door creak open. Benny lay very still, listening. But the cabin was quiet now.

Benny couldn't stay still another minute. He jumped out of bed and raced across the room to flip on the light switch.

"What's going on?" Henry sat straight up in bed, rubbing his eyes.

The cabin was flooded with light, and Benny pointed to the door. It was open!

"Someone was in here," Benny stammered. "Someone was here, in our cabin."

"Are you sure?"

"I'm positive." He jumped back in bed and pulled his knees up to his chest. Even though the danger was over, he still felt scared, and his teeth were chattering.

Henry crossed the floor and checked the solid pine door. "It could have been the wind," he said hesitantly. "But this is a pretty heavy door."

"It's not just the door!" Benny protested. "Something was moving all around the room. I heard it!" He looked around the room nervously. "Maybe it was a . . . ghost." He lowered his voice to a whisper. "Do you think that's possible?"

Henry peered around the open door and laughed. "Here's your ghost." Bingo darted into the room, barking happily.

"Bingo?" Benny said doubtfully. "Do you think that's what I heard?"

"It must have been." Henry reached down to pat the furry collie who immediately jumped onto the bed. "Maybe he was lonely and just wanted some company."

Benny wasn't convinced. "But how did he get the door open? And what was he doing under my bed?"

Henry watched as Benny scrambled under the bed and dragged out the cookie tin.

The top was half off, but his coin was safe. "Why would he be sniffing around a metal box?"

Henry shrugged. "I don't know. Maybe he remembered when it held cookies." Bingo jumped down and began nosing the tin. "See? It probably still smells like food to him."

"If you say so," Benny said, climbing back into bed.

Henry ushered Bingo out of the cabin and closed the door firmly behind him. "Let's get some sleep," he said, returning to his own bed.

"Okay, but I'm going to leave my light on," Benny said in a little voice. "Just in case."

The next morning, Henry went to the craft room after breakfast to drill a hole in Benny's coin. "How's that?" Henry said, holding it up. Soo Lee had given Benny a piece of jute to use as a cord, and Benny fastened the coin around his neck.

"Now I look like a real treasure hunter!" he said proudly.

Meanwhile, Jessie, Violet, and Soo Lee were sitting in the darkroom, watching as Melanie explained how to develop black-and-white photographs.

"After you put the prints in the final bath," she said, "you carefully lift them out of the solution with tongs and hang them to dry." She pointed to a long line that ran the length of the room. "You might want to take a look at the work that my advanced students have done. There's some beautiful underwater photography there."

"Oh, look at this one," Soo Lee said, pointing to a pretty sunset scene.

"That one was done by a professional," Melanie said. "Katherine Kelly took that photograph."

Violet walked over to the picture and stared at it for several seconds.

"What's the matter?" Jessie asked, noticing the serious expression on her face. "Don't you like it?"

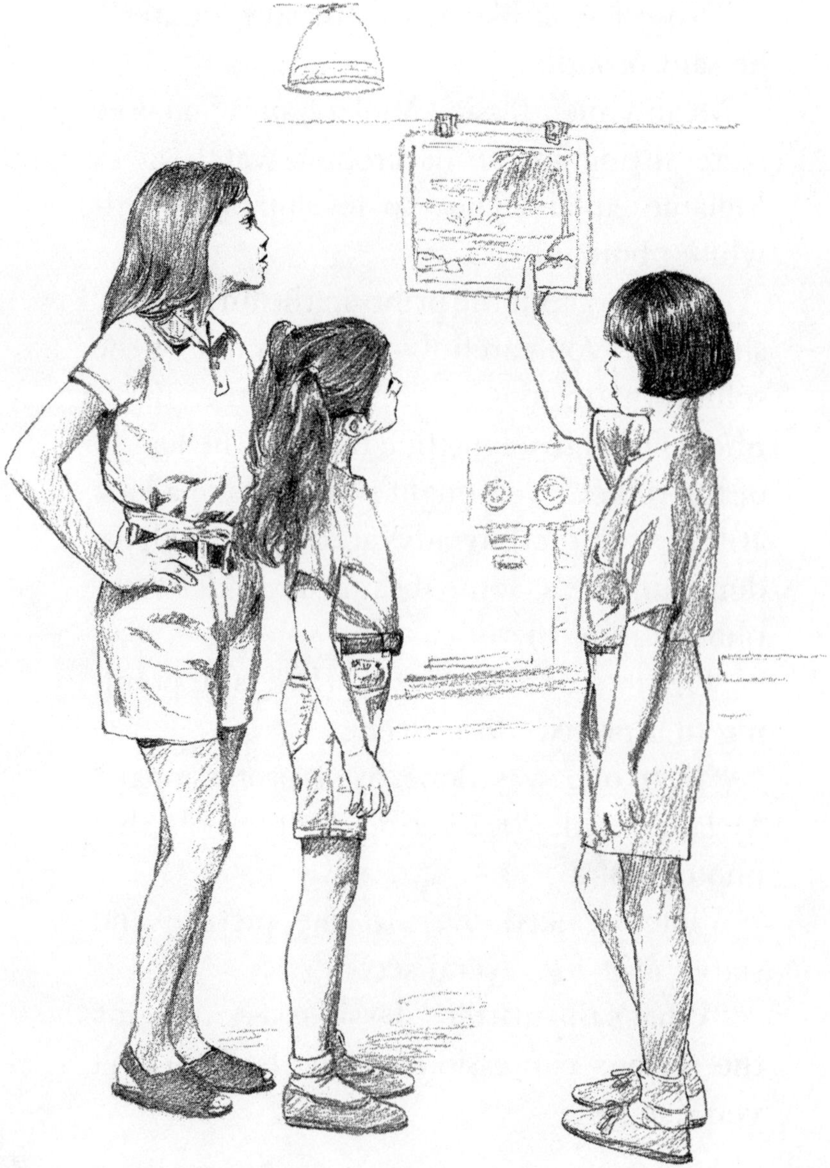

"Oh, yes, it's beautiful," Violet said. "But . . ."

"But what?" Soo Lee interrupted.

Violet shrugged. "I don't know. There's something about that picture. It looks so familiar."

"Maybe you saw it on a postcard," Jessie teased her. "You know, sunset, water, palm trees. Everywhere you look in Key West, you see the same scene."

Violet shook her head. "No, it's something else. It's more than that." Everyone left to have lunch then, but Violet couldn't resist taking a last look at the photograph. Why was the picture so disturbing? Where had she seen it before? She knew it was going to bother her until she remembered. She would just have to think.

Jessie came back to drag her out of the darkroom. "Hey, we're going to be last in the cafeteria line, if we don't get a move on. And they're having pizza today. They might run out!"

"I'm coming," Violet said reluctantly.

Jessie looked at the picture and shrugged. She wondered why Violet was so troubled by it. Jessie nudged her sister playfully. "Come on, Violet. You worry too much. Let's go eat!"

CHAPTER 8

The Thief Returns!

At lunch that day, Joshua Slade hurried to catch up with the children as they started to move through the cafeteria line.

"How are you doing today, Benny?" he asked cheerfully. "Did you have fun in Key West?"

"We saw some treasure from a shipwreck, and I got to hold a real gold bar," Benny told him. His eyes were fixed on the goodies in front of him. Should he have a hot dog or a grilled cheese sandwich?

Again, Henry wondered why the man was being so friendly. And something else made him suspicious. Joshua was leaning forward, craning his neck to get a view of Benny's neck. Why?

A moment later, the mystery was solved. "That's an interesting coin you're wearing, Benny. Is that the one you found down by the dock?"

Benny nodded, helping himself to a big bowl of chopped mangoes and papayas.

"Think I could look at it?" Joshua added. "I've always been interested in coins."

"Sure," Benny said absently. He held the coin away from his neck so Joshua could see it. "Henry drilled a hole in it for me. See, it's got a really nice design on it, and you can still read a few letters on the top — "

Joshua's eyes narrowed as he inspected the coin, and then he turned away, irritated. "Yeah, it's a great coin, kid." His voice was harsh. "See you later." He dropped his empty tray back in the rack and left the cafeteria abruptly.

Violet nudged Jessie. "What was that all about?"

"I don't know." Jessie glanced at Benny, who was reaching for a glass of milk. At least he didn't seem bothered by Joshua's rudeness.

"Joshua Slade acts very strange, don't you think?" Violet asked.

Jessie nodded. "Very strange. One minute he's friendly, and the next minute, he acts as if he doesn't like us."

As they ate lunch, Benny said he wanted to practice on the wind-surfing simulator that day.

"He's done a good job," Henry said to the girls. "Melanie said that we'll be able to go into the water soon."

"Shallow water," Melanie said, slipping into a seat beside him. "With life preservers."

Jessie nodded. At Camp Coral, safety always came first. "Have you heard anything new from the Coast Guard?" she asked Melanie.

"They don't have any leads yet," Melanie said regretfully. "I told Mr. Larson we'd all be on the look-out, but there's not much else we can do." She paused, and her eyes skimmed the crowded cafeteria. "Until the thief strikes again, of course."

"You think the thief will come back?" Benny's eyes were as big as saucers. He really wanted to catch the coral thief before they left camp. What a story this would be to tell Grandfather! They had solved dozens of mysteries in the past, and this might be the most exciting one of all.

"I'm sure he will," Melanie said grimly. "I just saw a new report on how much money people are getting for a boatload of coral. I bet the thief is greedy enough to try again."

"You think it's someone at camp, don't you?" Soo Lee asked. She had noticed the way Melanie had looked around the room moments earlier.

Melanie nodded. "It seems impossible, but yes, I do." She waved to a shy-looking young girl with a ponytail. "Excuse me," she said, pushing her chair back. "That's a new camper and she's feeling a little home-sick."

Everyone turned in early that night after a long, busy day out in the sun. Around midnight, Jessie awoke with a start. She heard a strange noise outside and sat straight up in bed, listening intently. *Putt-putt. Putt-putt.* "Someone's starting up a boat out there," she said softly. She knew it was against the camp's rules to take boats out at night.

She quickly woke her sister and Soo Lee. "Do you hear that noise?" she said, pointing to the open window. The noise had grown a little fainter, but could still be recognized.

"It's a boat," Soo Lee said sleepily.

"It sounds strange," Violet added. "It seems to skip a beat sometimes."

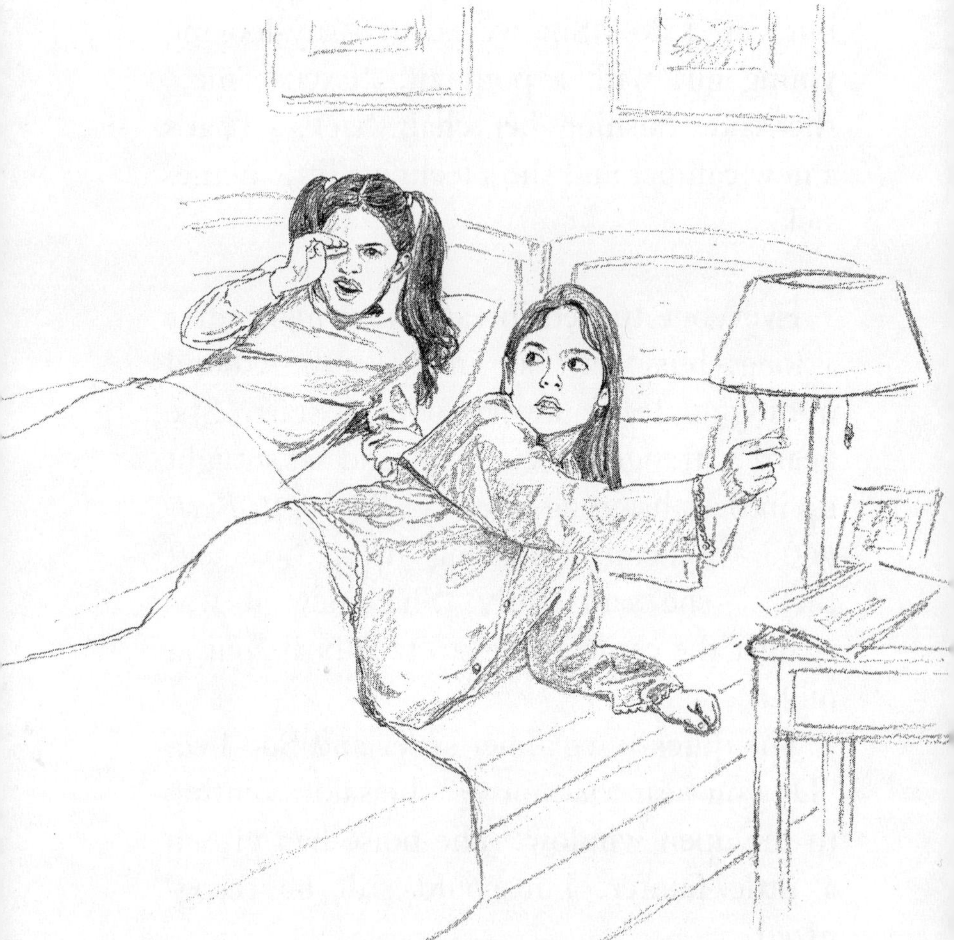

"Why is somebody out on the water at this time of night?" Jessie asked, pulling on her shorts.

"What are you doing?" Violet turned on the lamp next to her.

"Well, we can't just sit here listening," Jessie said impatiently. "It could be the coral thief. He could be out there stealing coral right this minute."

"Oh, no, you must be right," Violet said, scrambling out of bed. She struggled into a pair of jeans and reached for a flashlight. "Get dressed fast, Soo Lee. We need to do some investigating!"

"Let's get Henry and Benny," Soo Lee suggested.

"We'll have to hurry," Jessie said.

"I'm ready." Soo Lee had pulled on a pair of khaki shorts and a T-shirt.

They woke up the boys, and everyone hurried down the pathway to the dock. It was a balmy night, and a full moon made the bay look silvery. Even though it was warm, Jessie shivered a little.

"I think we're too late," Violet said when they reached the dock. The children stood silently, peering into the darkness. A bird called softly, but otherwise everything was still. The boat was nowhere in sight, and the engine noise had disappeared.

"Do you suppose he's sitting out there in the dark, and he cut the motor?" Henry asked. "Maybe he can see us standing here, and he's waiting for us to go back inside."

Jessie stared as hard as she could. There was absolutely no movement, no sign of anyone. "No," she said, disappointed. "I'm afraid there's nothing out there. He's just . . . gone."

"If only we had been quicker," Violet said.

"Maybe we can find some clues, just by looking around," Jessie suggested.

"Looking around here?" Benny asked doubtfully.

"You never know what may turn up. Let's walk along the dock before we give up," Jessie insisted.

They walked along the row of boats, each lost in thought.

"Look at that!" Soo Lee said suddenly. She pointed to an empty berth.

"Number six." Jessie grabbed Soo Lee's arm in excitement. "That's where that little white powerboat is always docked."

"So whoever is out on the water took it," Violet said.

"Unless they had permission to be out at night," Jessie said.

"I don't think so," Henry said. "Only the counselors have keys to the boats, and they don't go out at nighttime."

"Well, at least we learned something important tonight," Jessie said, as they headed back to their cabins. "We know someone was out on the water, and we know which boat they used. Tomorrow, we'll tell Melanie and decide what to do next."

CHAPTER 9

To Catch a Thief!

The next morning, the girls spotted Melanie in the cafeteria and told her about the mysterious boat they had heard during the night. "I'll have to report this," Melanie said. She looked very serious. "No one is allowed to take boats out at night — not even counselors." She paused, stirring her coffee. "And you're sure berth number six was vacant?"

Soo Lee nodded. "Yes."

"Well, whoever took the boat out returned

it," Melanie said. "I was down at the docks half an hour ago, and all the berths were filled."

Benny came racing into the cafeteria just then, followed by Henry. "We're getting closer and closer to the thief," Benny said.

"Maybe not," Violet said doubtfully. "Maybe he got everything he wanted last night, and he won't show up again."

After breakfast, the Aldens decided to take a quick look at the docks. Maybe they could find a clue they had missed the night before. As they strolled along the docks, Benny stared hard at the powerboat docked in berth number six. It looked absolutely normal — white fiberglass finish, a wood-grain dashboard, blue vinyl seats. . . .

Suddenly he stopped dead in his tracks. There was something shiny lying on one of the seats. What was it? It was so small it would fit in the palm of his hand, and it glinted in the morning sun. He tugged urgently on Henry's arm. "Look at the seat!"

he said in a hushed voice. "What is it? Can you reach it?"

Henry used one hand to steady himself and quickly stepped inside the boat. He scooped up the bright object and was back on the dock in a flash.

"What is it?" Benny was nearly jumping up and down in excitement.

"A clue," Henry said, opening his hand. Everyone crowded around to look at a small gold cigarette lighter. It was initialed with the letters NS. "Probably a very important clue."

"NS," Violet said thoughtfully. She and Jessie exchanged a look. "Nick Simon!" they said in unison.

"I think he's just moved to the top of our list of suspects," Benny said.

That evening, the counselors took some of the campers to Bird Island for a cookout. The Aldens rode in a large boat, and Melanie rowed across the bay in a rowboat.

"That looks like fun," Benny said, watching as Melanie smoothly guided the rowboat through the water.

"You certainly did a good job on the wind-surfing simulator," Jessie said. "Grandfather will be proud of you. We'll be seeing him tomorrow, you know."

"Tomorrow?"

"We've been here a whole week," Violet reminded him. "The time went fast because we've been doing so much."

"And learning so many new things," Soo Lee added.

"I wish we could stay longer," Benny said. "I never got to use the real wind-surfer. The kind that goes in the water."

Violet put her arm around him. "Maybe next time, Benny."

After dinner, everyone sang songs and toasted marshmallows around a campfire. Soo Lee had never tasted marshmallows before, and Benny showed her how to thread them on a stick and hold them over the flames.

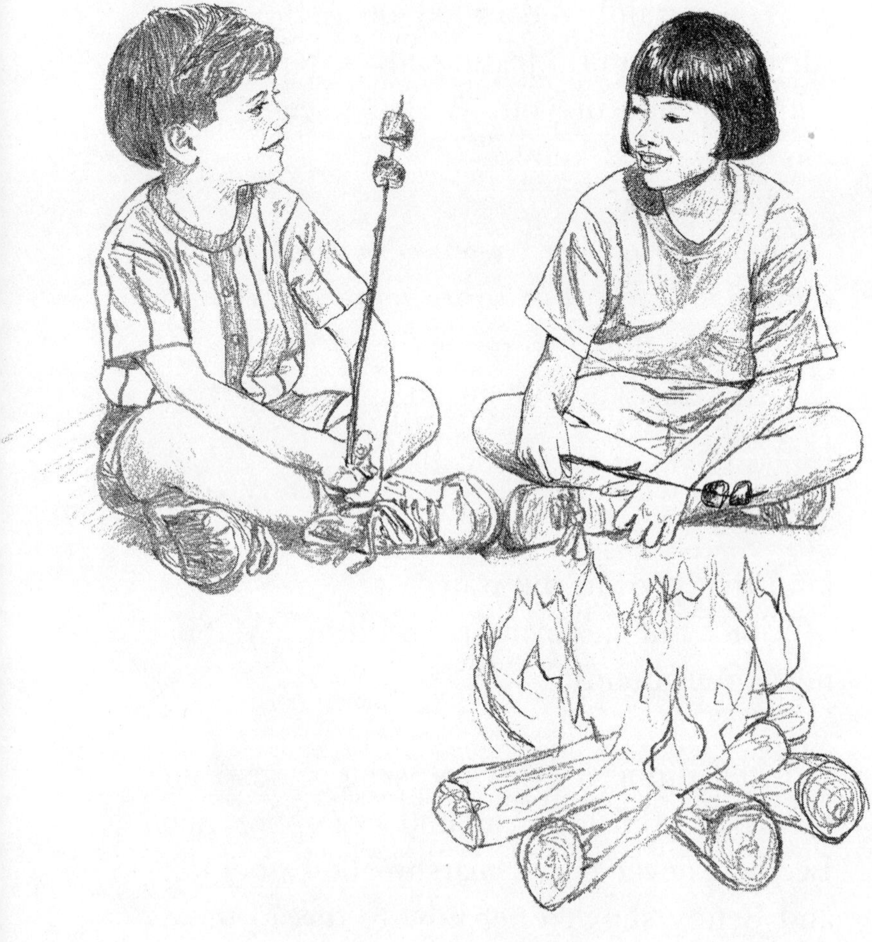

"Mmmm!" she said when she'd tried her first toasted marshmallow. "This is great!" Violet felt a little sad because she knew she would miss the camp, and especially Melanie, who had become a good friend. And worst of all, they had never solved the mystery of the missing coral!

"Are you thinking the same thing I am?" Jessie said quietly. She had caught the look on her sister's face as she stared into the fire.

Violet nodded. "Probably. I've been thinking about the coral thief — who he is, what he's planning to do next. This is the first time we've come up against a mystery we couldn't solve."

Jessie sighed. "I know. All we can do is hope that the thief slips up somehow, and Melanie catches him after we leave."

A little later, the counselors suggested a hike around the island, but the Aldens decided to stay at the campfire. The sun had already set in a blaze of fiery orange, and the night air was soft and balmy.

"It's so peaceful here," Jessie said. "I want

to sit and watch the stars come out one by one."

"I want to watch the moonlight," Violet said. "It looks so pretty when it shines on the water."

"And I want to watch the campfire," Benny said. "We still have another whole package of marshmallows left!"

Everyone laughed, and the group began hiking along the shore, leaving the Aldens alone.

Darkness spread across the island very quickly, and half an hour later, Benny was startled to see a flashing light on the water. It was at the far end of the island, but he could see it clearly, twinkling in the distance. He stood up, curious, and then he heard a familiar sound. *Putt-putt. Putt-putt.*

"There's that boat again," Violet said in a hushed voice. "I know it!"

Henry and the girls scrambled to their feet. "How can you be so sure?" Henry asked.

"Because it's the same boat we heard a couple of nights ago," she insisted.

"Don't all powerboats sound alike?" Henry asked.

"This one's different," Violet said, shaking her head. "It skips a *putt* every now and then. I know it's the same one we heard before. Boat number six."

"You're right," Henry agreed. "Melanie said that the boat has a bad transmission, and that's why it skips every so often."

"What can we do?" Jessie asked eagerly.

Suddenly the *putt-putt* sound stopped, and the Aldens stood motionless, straining to hear.

"Why has the noise stopped?" Benny whispered.

"I don't know — " Violet started to say, and then stopped. All at once she realized what was going on. "Oh, no!" she cried. "The thief has docked the boat. What if he's going to steal more coral?"

"We have to get Melanie and .the other

counselors," Henry said. "And we need to move fast."

"They've been gone for a while," Jessie said. "How will we find them?"

"We'll have to split up," Henry said. "Violet, you and I will take the rowboat to the other end of the island. At least we'll know what's going on, and we may even get a look at the thief."

"Soo Lee and I can try to find the campers," Jessie said.

"Don't walk along the shoreline. It will take too long," Henry pointed out.

"We'll cut through the woods instead," Soo Lee said quickly. She scrambled to her feet, glad that she had worn long pants and sturdy shoes.

"Hey," Benny said. "How about me?"

"You're coming with us," Henry said, grabbing his hand.

"Good — there are three life jackets inside," Violet said when they reached the rowboat a couple of minutes later. They quickly put them on, and Henry helped Violet and Benny into the rear seat. Then he lowered himself into the middle seat and took up the oars.

When they had almost reached the shore at the other end of the island, Benny heard a sharp sound. "What's that?" he asked.

"I bet the thief is using a hammer on the coral bed," Henry said in disgust. "We'll have to hurry."

They docked the rowboat as quietly as they could and crept cautiously along the hard-packed sand. The beach was very dark, but suddenly they saw a light dancing at the edge of the water, just a few yards away.

"That light's moving all by itself!" Benny said in a shaky voice.

"No, there's a person holding it," Violet said. She grabbed Benny's hand and held it tightly. "Someone's coming out of the water and he's all dressed in black. That's why you can't see him."

"He's wearing a wetsuit," Henry whispered. They inched a little closer. Violet noticed that the person was slim, and carrying a big chunk of coral. A snorkel mask covered most of his face.

"Who is it?" Benny asked, edging close to Violet.

She shook her head. "I can't tell yet. Let's see what he does."

They watched as the dark figure lifted the coral into a powerboat docked nearby and went back into the water.

"He's after more coral!" Violet said angrily. "We have to stop him!"

"I know," Henry said, "but we need help. Can you stay here and try to get a look at his face? I'm going to take the rowboat and find the others."

"Be quick," Benny said.

"Don't worry, I will," Henry assured them.

He darted back to the rowboat, just as the thief emerged from the water. After dropping another load of coral in the powerboat, the figure in the wet suit stopped to rest for a moment.

"What's he doing now?" Benny whispered.

"I don't know — " Violet started to say, and then stopped. The figure had pulled off his snorkel mask, and Violet nearly gasped in surprise. It was Katherine Kelly!

She started to inch backward, still clutching Benny by the hand, when he gave a sharp yelp of pain.

"Oh, Benny," Violet said. She didn't want Katherine to see them.

"I'm sorry," he said in a little voice. "I stepped on a shell."

Katherine's head swung around at the sound, but before she could spot them, Violet ran into the woods and pulled Benny behind a giant banyan tree.

Suddenly an arm appeared out of the darkness. It grabbed Violet by the shoulder and she almost screamed.

"It's okay," a calm voice said. "It's only me." When the man stepped closer, she recognized his face.

"Nick Simon?" she asked doubtfully.

What was he doing in the woods at night?

"There's nothing to be afraid of," Nick said. Violet wasn't sure if she could believe him.

"What's going on?" Henry's voice boomed out.

"We're over here!" Violet called out. Her brother was at her side in a second.

"I was just stepping into the boat when I heard Benny cry out," Henry said. Then he looked at Nick. "What are you doing here?"

"I'm here for the same reason you are. To catch the coral thief."

Henry hesitated. Was Nick telling the truth? Up until now, he had been one of the main suspects.

"He's not the thief!" Benny blurted out. "It's Katherine Kelly. We saw her!"

"Where is she?" Nick asked.

"She's down at the beach," Violet said.

"That's all I need to know," Nick said. He took a walkie-talkie out of his pocket and spoke a few words. When he finished talking, he smiled at the children. "They'll pick her up in a few minutes. We have officers all over the island."

"Officers?" Jessie said in surprise. "You're with the police?"

"Detective Nick Simon," he answered, pulling out his badge. "I've been working undercover for months, trying to get a lead on the thief. But you're the ones who really solved the crime," he told them. "I knew it was someone at Camp Coral, but I couldn't figure out who."

"Neither could we," Henry said. "We even suspected you."

"Are you sure the police will get there in time?" Violet said worriedly. "All she has to do is jump in the powerboat and get away."

"Not without this, she won't." Henry held up a thin wire. "She can't get far with her spark plugs disconnected."

Nick laughed. "You'd make good detectives."

CHAPTER 10

The Mystery Is Solved!

"That about wraps it up, Nick," a pale man with sandy hair said a few minutes later. He was standing at the edge of the shore, watching as another officer handcuffed Katherine Kelly, and helped her into a police patrol boat.

"I know you!" Benny said. "I met you with Nick in Key West. He said you were a fisherman."

Nick laughed. "This is Officer Adams, Benny. I'm afraid I had to tell a little white

lie. I couldn't explain that we're both undercover investigators."

"What's going to happen now?" Henry
asked. He glanced at Katherine Kelly, who
glared back at him.

"It's an airtight case." Officer Adams
pointed to a group of men in Coast Guard
uniforms who were carefully placing the
stolen coral in clear plastic bags. "We've got
eyewitnesses, we've got the stolen coral, and
we've got the tools she used."

"It sounds like you caught her in the act,"
Nick said.

Officer Adams nodded. "We did. She
had just dumped another load in her boat.
It's funny, but she couldn't get the engine started. That was a lucky break for
us."

Nick laughed as Henry held up the wire.
"It was more than just a lucky break. Henry
disconnected her spark plugs. She'd be miles
away by now, without the help of my young
friends."

Jessie and Soo Lee appeared just then,

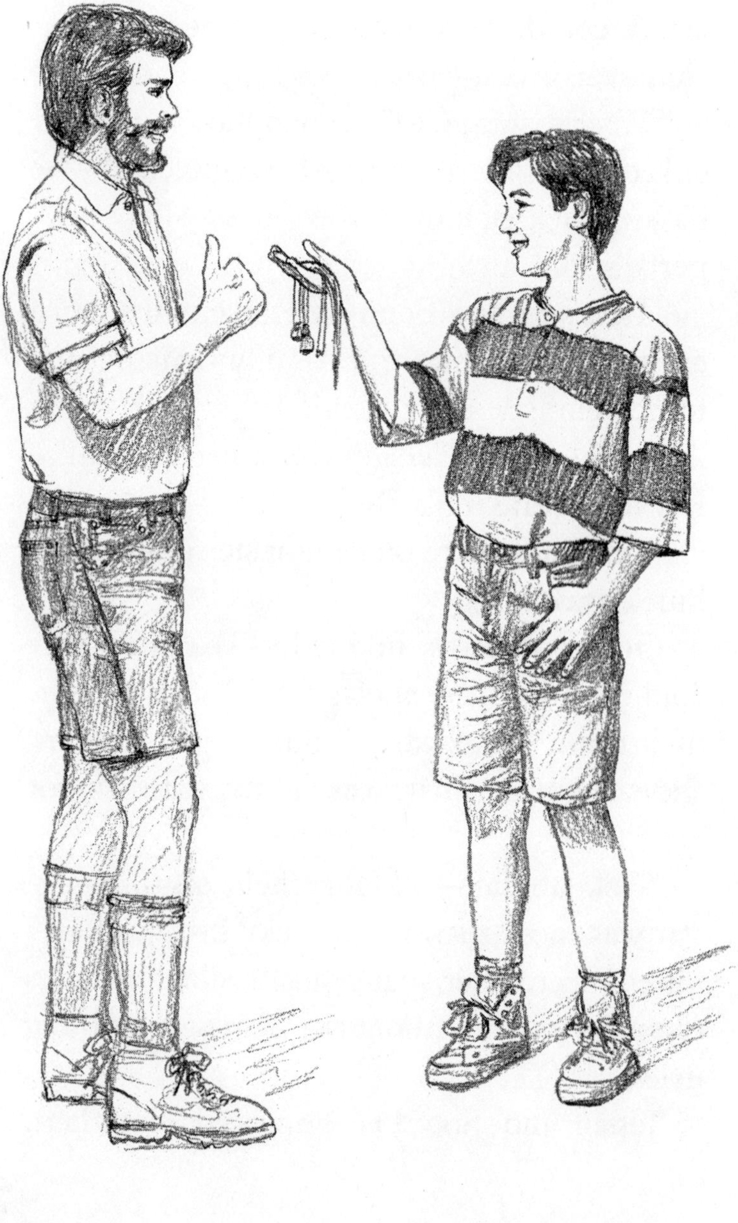

followed by a group of counselors and campers.

"What's going on?" Jessie asked, and then gasped as she spotted Katherine Kelly in handcuffs. "She was the one?" she whispered.

"That's right," Benny said excitedly. "We caught her stealing the coral and we recognized her when she took her face mask off. And then — we had to run into the woods! It was scary!"

"I'm glad you're okay," Jessie said, giving him a quick hug.

"Someone better fill me in," Melanie said, coming up behind Jessie. She was out of breath. "We heard the noise and ran all the way back from the other side of the island."

Nick smiled. "Well, the bottom line is that the kids solved the crime for us. Without them, Katherine might have made one last haul, and then disappeared for good."

"But I don't understand," Jessie said. She

turned to Nick. "You're not really a marine biologist?"

Violet laughed. "He's a police officer, but it's a long story."

"I have a lot of questions, too," Melanie said. "How about if we all go back to Camp Coral and discuss it?"

Half an hour later, everyone met at the picnic tables down by the dock at the camp. The other officers had left the island, but Nick stayed behind to talk about the case. Melanie lit some tiki lamps, and the campers and counselors gathered close to ask questions.

"Was she really an underwater photographer?" Soo Lee asked.

"Yes, she was a real photographer. Her work has been featured in some big magazines." Nick paused. "I guess she just decided she could make more money from stealing coral."

"It was the picture! That's what made me wonder!" Violet blurted out. Everyone turned to look at her. "Katherine took a really pretty picture of a sunset and we saw it hanging to dry in the darkroom."

"I remember how much that picture bothered you," Jessie said. "But I never understood why."

"I didn't either — until now." She turned to Melanie. "There was something about the rock, and the sunset that looked so familiar. I realized that I had seen that exact same view before — from your private island!"

"So the only way Katherine could have gotten that picture was if she had been standing in the same spot we were," Jessie said slowly. "She probably discovered the big coral bed that day and decided to chop away at it."

"It will take hundreds of years to grow back," Melanie said sadly.

"Don't feel bad, Melanie," Violet said, edging close to her. "At least she'll never be able to do it again."

"When did you first suspect her?" A male voice came from the back of the crowd.

Henry turned to see Joshua Slade raising his hand.

"Right from the start," Nick answered. "But I suspected a lot of people. You and your wife, for example."

Hilary Slade laughed nervously. "Surely you didn't suspect us."

"I certainly did. You two don't know much about sailing for a couple who are supposed to run a charter business."

"That's right!" Soo Lee agreed. "You didn't even recognize a square knot when I showed you my macrame piece."

"And you stuffed a fish inside your shirt!" Benny piped up. "I saw you that night we were out collecting specimens."

"I stuffed a what? Oh, now I get it." Joshua laughed. "That wasn't a fish. I thought I saw a rare coin in the water, and I scooped it up and hid it in my shirt. I didn't think anyone saw me."

"You're interested in rare coins?" Henry said. "So that was you snooping around our cabin that night!"

Joshua looked embarrassed. "I'm afraid it was. To tell the truth, we're treasure hunters, not sailors.

"From the way he talked, I thought Benny had found a doubloon. I didn't realize it was worthless." He paused. "The only valuable thing I found here was the conch shell and it was cracked."

"You took my conch shell?" Violet asked.

Joshua looked embarrassed, realizing his slip. "I wanted to show it one of my investors. I wasn't sure how rare it really was."

"What did you do with it?" Melanie asked.

"I stuffed it in a drawer in the classroom," Joshua said defiantly. "I figured you'd find it eventually."

Everyone was silent for a moment, and then Jessie spoke up. "We even suspected you, Nick. Someone took a powerboat out one night, and we found a key ring with the initials NS lying on the seat."

"I can explain that," Nick said. "NS stands for North Star. They're a big coral wholesaler. Those are probably the people that Katherine was dealing with."

Violet reached down to pet the tabby cat who was rubbing against her legs. "At least we know now that Horace didn't scratch Katherine." She saw the surprised look on Nick's face. "Her legs were all scratched from the mangrove trees on Melanie's island, and she blamed it on poor Horace."

"Breaking into someone's cabin is against camp rules," Melanie said sternly to Joshua Slade. "You won't be welcome here again."

"I'm sorry about that," Joshua said softly. He looked at his wife and they turned and walked back to their cabin.

"All those times they acted friendly," Violet remarked, "they were just trying to see if we knew about any sunken treasure."

Benny stifled a yawn. "I can't believe the mystery is all solved," he said sleepily.

"And just in time," Violet said. She glanced at her watch. "Grandfather will be here in just a few hours to pick us up."

"You did a great job, kids," Nick said.

He stepped through the crowd to shake hands with each of them. "Without you, Katherine could have moved on to other sites and other coral beds. It might have taken months, or even years, to catch up with her."

"I'm glad we could help," Henry said. He looked at Benny, who was leaning against him with his eyes half closed. "But now I think it's time to say good night. My little brother is sleeping standing up."

"I'm awake," Benny protested drowsily. As soon as Henry lifted him up, Benny's eyes shut and he snuggled against his older brother.

"Good night," Melanie said softly. "I'll see you in the morning before you leave. Let's have breakfast together."

Grandfather arrived bright and early the following morning. "I'm so glad to see you!" he said, hugging Violet, Jessie, Henry, and Soo Lee. They were already packed and waiting by the camp entrance.

"We spent days out on the water," Jessie said. "It was wonderful."

"But where's Benny?" Grandfather asked, looking around.

"He's here," Violet said playfully. "He's down by the shore. He has something special he wants to show you." She took Grandfather's hand. "Come on, I'll take you there."

"Whatever you say," Grandfather said good-naturedly. He was so happy to see his grandchildren. He missed them, even if they were only away for a few days.

"Tell us about your trip, Grandfather," Henry said.

"It was very relaxing," Grandfather began. "I did a little sailing and I — " He broke off suddenly as they approached the beach. "Is that Benny?"

"It sure is!" Jessie said proudly.

All the children watched as a small figure skimmed over the water on a bright red wind-surfer.

Henry whistled under his breath. "He really got the hang of it," he said admiringly.

"He wanted you to be proud of him, Grandfather."

"Well, I am," Mr. Alden replied, waving to Benny as he zigzagged toward the shore. "I'm proud of all my grandchildren." He moved forward to greet Benny as he neared the shore. "And what have the rest of you been doing while Benny learned wind-surfing? Did anything special happen?"

Violet and Jessie exchanged a look and burst out laughing. "Anything special! Grandfather, we solved another mystery!"

"Tell me about it," he said as Benny ran along the sand toward him.

"It will take a long time," Soo Lee pointed out. "It's a long story."

Grandfather gave Benny a bear hug and scooped him up in his arms. "That's all right," he said, heading back to the car. "We have a long drive back to the Miami airport. But nothing will make the time go faster than hearing about your adventures!"

GERTRUDE CHANDLER WARNER discovered when she was teaching that many readers who like an exciting story could find no books that were both easy and fun to read. She decided to try to meet this need, and her first book, *The Boxcar Children*, quickly proved she had succeeded.

Miss Warner drew on her own experiences to write the mystery. As a child she spent hours watching trains go by on the tracks opposite her family home. She often dreamed about what it would be like to set up housekeeping in a caboose or freight car — the situation the Alden children find themselves in.

When Miss Warner received requests for more adventures involving Henry, Jessie, Violet, and Benny Alden, she began additional stories. In each, she chose a special setting and introduced unusual or eccentric characters who liked the unpredictable.

While the mystery element is central to each of Miss Warner's books, she never thought of them as strictly juvenile mysteries. She liked to stress the Aldens' independence and resourcefulness and their solid New England devotion to using up and making do. The Aldens go about most of their adventures with as little adult supervision as possible — something else that delights young readers.

Miss Warner lived in Putnam, Connecticut, until her death in 1979. During her lifetime, she received hundreds of letters from girls and boys telling her how much they liked her books.